His Inconvenient Choice

A PRIDE AND PREJUDICE VARIATION

LEENIE BROWN

Leenie B Books
Halifax

Copyright

Dedication

In honour of the man whose encouragement and love have
led to my foray into publishing

~*~

You will always be my choice.
I will always choose you.

Chapter 1

JANUARY 1, 1812

THE CARRIAGE DOOR CLOSED. It was over. His happy sojourn in Hertfordshire was over. Mr. and Mrs. Bingley were married, as were Lord and Lady Rycroft — their breakfast was nearing its end.

The conveyance in which Colonel Richard Fitzwilliam sat lurched into motion and rolled down Netherfield's drive, moving his person towards town and leaving his heart behind.

He unfolded the small piece of paper that had been tucked into his pocket as he had left the wedding breakfast and shook his head. Two cousins and a friend newly married and all within the space of two weeks was enough to set anyone's world on end. It was also the sort of thing that made Richard contemplate his own future.

As always, such thoughts made breathing become something one had to strain to do. As quietly as he could, Richard drew a slow, deep breath and hoped that with his exhalation the feeling of being crushed would also leave his body.

However, his attempt was only slightly successful. The truth of the matter was that there was no way to remove all the crushing oppression that thoughts of his future brought, for his future could never be so happy as those of his cousins and Bingley. He was not free to choose where he wished. He did not have complete control over his destiny and fortune. His marriage would be one of convenience; his father would see to that.

Not wishing to draw attention to it from the others in the carriage, he looked surreptitiously at the paper in his palm. The drawing there brought a smile to his lips and a pang of regret to his heart. Forget-me-nots graced the lid of a box from which spilled strands of pearls and chains of gold. He refolded the drawing again and slipped it back into his pocket.

If his heart could make his choice for him instead of his father, Kitty Bennet would be his choice. She had stolen his heart while she stood, shivering in the wind, on the street in front of the milliner's shop on Meryton's high street as she had insisted on being introduced to him as Katherine.

Upon further acquaintance, she had proven to be a lady who shared many of his same interests and who made him feel at ease. She expected no more from him than for him to be himself. He did not need to be a military leader or the son of an earl. She cared for none of that.

She had even been interested in his wooden creations — and not as a lady who was trying to make a favourable impression on a gentleman might be. No, Katherine had listened with interest and animation when he had told her about his love of creating with wood. She had even sketched a few designs that he might like to use.

"If you could wait but a year," she had said as they had strolled the perimeter of the ballroom last night, "then your inheritance will be yours."

He had felt her hopefulness and had longed to be able to enter into it with her, but he knew the reality of the situation.

"He will not allow me to be free. He will insist on my marrying before he gives me one farthing more than I have," he had replied.

Her eyes had filled with tears that she had refused to shed, and his heart had broken a bit more at both the thought of a life without her and the knowledge that his father was the source of her pain.

"If I could wait," he had whispered, "I would wait a thousand years for you."

She had smiled sadly at him and said, "And I would wait for you."

He once again ran his gloved finger over the drawing in the pocket of his coat.

"Do not forget me," she had said as she had slipped it into his pocket when he was taking his leave of her.

He knew he would never forget her. He could not. She was burned into his heart forever.

His hand closed around the paper.

"You are looking rather pensive, Colonel," Caroline Bingley said, interrupting his thoughts. "Are they pleasant things that occupy your mind?"

"Not all of them." He turned to look out the window, hoping she would take the action for what it was meant to be – an end to their discussion.

If the weather had not been so foul, he would have refused Hurst's offer to travel with him. Being held captive in a carriage with a lady the likes of Caroline Bingley was not something he wished to do on a day when his heart was not a tattered, mangled mess. Today, the prospect was even less welcome.

"That is a pity," Louisa Hurst said. "I prefer to think on agreeable things whenever possible."

"As do I," Richard said, "but it is not always possible."

"A colonel must have many disagreeable things to consider," Miss Bingley added.

Richard did not turn from his contemplation of the dreary dampness of the day outside the carriage window.

"Indeed, he must," he replied, "and I often do."

Had her fortune been from land rather than trade, Miss Bingley might be of some value to his father. If she had relations in parliament or who were friends of someone who was in parliament, that also would be a mark in her favour, and with those two most important items attached to her name – money from a proper source and some social standing of significance – she might stand a chance of becoming his bride. Not that Richard would ever chose her of his own accord, but his father would.

"However," he continued, "I was not thinking as a colonel just now but rather as a mere man."

Hurst snorted at the comment. "Do leave him be, Caroline."

Hurst was the husband of Miss Bingley's sister and not more than two years Richard's elder. He was also not someone who would meet with Lord Matlock's approval. Oh, his clothes would. For they were always the latest style. His bank account and connections, however, were not as becoming. That is not to say he was poor, but he also was not notably wealthy among the upper circles in town.

"I was only attempting to pass the time in conversation," she replied with a huff. "The light is too poor for anything else."

"I find a quiet nap a most refreshing way to pass a trip," Hurst replied.

"How dull," Miss Bingley grumbled.

"Not at all," Richard countered. "I find I would like to close my eyes. It has been a busy two days."

Hurst nodded. "It has been, and you were out with your men yesterday morning, were you not?"

"I put them through a few drills to test them." Richard turned to his bench mate. "Those who passed my test were allowed to attend the ball last night. Those who did not pass were confined to quarters for the evening."

It had been his plan, and a successful one, to keep Wickham from the ball. He would take every opportunity afforded him by his position while he held it to ensure that Wickham had less enjoyment than he desired. It was one of the few pleasures Richard received from his duty.

"And, I believe, you danced every dance, did you not?" Mrs. Hurst asked.

"All save one." His heart pinched, for that one had been set aside to stroll with Kitty.

"Oh, Hurst, you are right. I do believe a nap must be had. What with an early morning yesterday for the colonel, a night of dancing, and another early start to the day today, he must be very tired." She turned to her sister. "It would be most unkind of us to keep him from his rest."

"I thank you," Richard said with a bow of his head before Miss Bingley could say a word to either agree or disagree with her sister. "I am indeed rather tired," he added as he settled back and closed his eyes.

His fingers once again sought that slip of paper in his pocket. Finding it, he allowed his mind to wander to the lady who had given it to him, and with a deep exhale, he attempted to find some peace in sleep.

~*~

Katherine Bennet turned from the window where she had been watching the Hursts' carriage drive away. Her stomach fluttered anxiously, and she wanted to do anything but what she knew she must. There were not many wedding guests remaining, and she knew that both she and the Darcys would leave soon. Then, her opportunity to do what was needed would become nearly impossible, barring a visit to town and Darcy House. She pressed her hand against her stomach, trying to calm the flutters. She could do this. For him, she could do this.

"Mr. Darcy, may I have a word with you?" she said.

"Certainly," her brother-in-law replied with a smile that helped ease her mind the tiniest bit. Still, she could not keep from twisting her fingers together in front of her stomach and biting her lip.

Mr. Darcy's presence always unsettled her. He almost always looked serious. She was sure that he was, at any moment, going to scold her for some foolishness. She knew she had no reason to feel so beyond his sometimes-severe expression, but she did. And what she wished to speak to him about at present was something that could earn her a look of displeasure or more.

She barely resisted the urge to duck her head and hide from him. "I have a little bit of money and expect to receive some more."

She reminded herself that Mr. Darcy was the person who was best be able to advise her about her money and straightened her shoulders before continuing.

"I have sold some dress designs to Mrs. Havelston, and she has requested some more. I have not signed them with my name, and it is to be a secret arrangement." The words rushed from her. "I would like to invest the money she pays me. I know that you can earn money with money, but I do not know how to do it, and I am not a gentleman, which limits me."

He smiled at her. "That sounds like a wise thing to do."

Her brows drew together. "It does?" She had not expected him to commend her for her idea.

"Indeed." He was still smiling at her, so she returned the expression before withdrawing a small velvet pouch from her reticule.

"It is really very little. Just a few pounds. It may not even be enough to invest yet, but I dare not place it in my father's strongbox, for if something happens to him, I do not wish to explain how I came to have this money to Mr. Collins."

Darcy took the bag from her and slipped it into his pocket. "I shall care for it for you. You will keep a record of what you have given me, and I will do the same. Do you know how to do this?"

She pursed her lips and drew her brows together. It was likely similar to keeping a balance for household expenses, but she wasn't sure exactly how it was different. "I will have my father or my uncle show me since I am not entirely certain that I do."

"That sounds like an excellent idea."

That was twice now that he had commended her. It was an extraordinarily wonderful feeling, but she had not presented the whole situation to him.

"Mr. Darcy, could we save some time and trouble if I were to request that my uncle give the money to you?" She twisted her hands again. She could not help it. She was still nervous, though her nerves had shifted from worrying about Mr. Darcy scolding her to someone discovering that she was earning money by selling designs.

"Uncle Gardiner regularly receives payments from Mrs. Havelston for her orders of cloth," she explained, "so no one would suspect she is paying me if she includes my payment with her payment to him. And if he were to meet with you, no one would question the activity."

He tipped his head and looked at her closely but not as if looking to criticize. It was as if he were seeing her for the first time. "You have thought this through very thoroughly."

"I have to. If anyone was to learn that I was earning money…" Her reputation might be damaged and that would reflect poorly on her sisters as well. She could not risk that.

"I understand. It is to be a secret arrangement. I would be happy to have Mr. Gardiner deliver your money to me," Mr. Darcy said. "Do you have a plan in mind for it?"

Oh, how she wished he had not asked that! The tears that had been threatening all morning sprang to her eyes, and her cheeks flushed in embarrassment.

"You do not have to tell me," Mr. Darcy said in a quiet, gentle voice.

She shook her head. "No, you should know since you are helping me." She drew a steadying breath. "I have a foolish notion that will probably be unsuccessful, but your cousin should not be forced to give up what he loves. I thought perhaps... eventually... I could help him find a way to be happy." She shrugged. "If not, then the money can be added to my portion, which will be of assistance to me when I need to set up my own establishment. I do not wish to live solely on the charity of my relations."

"You do not plan to marry?" Darcy asked in surprise.

The tears once again gathered in her eyes, and she blinked against them as she shook her head. "I had hoped to," she said softly as her gaze shifted toward the window and the drive where her father's carriage stood before the door.

"One must not lose hope, Miss Kitty. Circumstances can change."

She drew another a deep breath and released it slowly. Then, she gave him as much of a smile as she could manage. "While I own that it is not an utter impossibility, I think it highly unlikely."

Chapter 2

THE SUN WAS SINKING close to the horizon by the time Richard exited Hurst's carriage and entered Matlock House. He stripped off his greatcoat and handed it, along with his hat, to Mr. Harrison, the butler. Then, he slipped quietly into his mother's sitting room to greet her.

"I am happy to see you safely returned to me," Lady Matlock said as she held him close in a firm embrace. "Will you be staying?" She smoothed the front of his jacket. Then, she took a seat on a settee and motioned for him to join her.

"I have no choice," he said as he sat down next to her. "I do not wish to impose on Darcy or Rycroft as they are settling in with their wives." If he had a choice, he would not be here for more than a few minutes to see her. He would rather avoid his father.

"There is BayLeafe."

He shook his head at the offer. BayLeafe was the small estate just outside of town which was part of the inheritance to come to him through his mother, should his father see fit to give it to him. That estate was no more his home than the grand townhouse in which he sat now. Home should be a place where you felt at ease. That was not Matlock House, nor was it any of his father's other properties.

"Your father is in quite a state, what with both of your cousins marrying outside of what is proper." She reached up and brushed his hair back from his forehead. "He is not all bad, you know. He has been good to me. He is just set in his ways."

"Do you love him?" Richard's voice was soft.

"I suppose I do," she replied. "It is possible to become friends and then more even when you begin as near strangers." She took his hand. "I cannot say I have never wished for more or for another, for I did at first, but now, I cannot imagine my life in any other way."

Richard nodded and placed the small, folded drawing in her hand. "You would have liked her," he said as his mother unfolded the paper.

Where his father blustered, his mother spoke softly. Where his father was arrogant, she demonstrated grace and humility. They were, in many ways, as opposed as darkness and light.

She lay the drawing on her lap and rested a hand on her heart. "It is very well done. Who is she?"

He shook his head and took the paper from her lap. "It matters not, for it shall never be." He rose and went to the window. "She has neither wealth nor significant connections beyond our family."

Lady Matlock came to stand near him. "Is she connected to our family?"

He nodded. "Her sisters are the new Mrs. Darcy and Lady Rycroft." He turned toward her. "And that is not the worst of it. A third sister is the new Mrs. Bingley."

He watched his mother struggle with how to accept this information. He knew she loved him and would wish him only to be happy, but she also held to some of the same ideas regarding marriage as her husband. It was not only his father who wished for him to make a good match.

He tucked the paper in his pocket. "As I said, it matters not, for it shall never be. My heart is of little importance."

Raised voices could be heard coming from somewhere down the hall.

"Your aunt is here," his mother said in answer to his questioning look. "Anne is with her but has taken to her room;, whether it is due to ill health or a need to avoid her mother, I am uncertain."

Just then, Lady Catherine stomped into the sitting room. "He is as unreasonable as ever!"

"I am not being unreasonable," Lord Matlock retorted as he followed his sister into the room. "You are being daft. To accept such connections into the family without some censure? And after Darcy did not marry Anne as we had planned?" He threw his hands up as if unable to fathom the thoughts.

"It would be better for Anne to marry someone with higher connections," Lady Catherine said, "a peer or the son of a peer." Her eyes came to rest on Richard. "Even a second son would do."

Richard attempted to keep his expression neutral, but marry Anne? No, he had no desire to marry Anne.

A sly smile spread slowly across Lord Matlock's face. "That is an idea worthy of contemplation. It would keep all the land holding within the family." He clapped his hands together and rubbed them back and forth. "I shall have my solicitor draw up the arrangement. Shall we have the wedding in two months? I do think that would give enough time to find the colonel a replacement with his unit and ready the necessary items for the release of his inheritance. However, I will have to defer to my solicitor and man of business for advice before we finalize the date." He leveled a hard glare at Richard. "Any objection shall be met with a significant, if not permanent, breach. Do I make myself clear?"

Richard shook his head in disbelief. "Am I no more to you than that? Some hireling to be ordered about?"

"On the contrary," his father said. "You are of great significance, and that is why your future must be secured. If something were to ever happen to your brother, you would need to secure the title with an appropriate heir, one with an acceptable lineage."

Richard's jaw clenched. "Ah, so I am not a hireling but, rather, a well-bred horse in your stable, whose only expectation is to sire the next prize stallion. And, doubtlessly, if I do not, I, like that horse, shall be turned out to work alongside the other workhorses on the estate."

His father's eyes narrowed. "Not on my estates." His voice held more than a little warning.

Richard stepped closer and pulled himself up to his full height, which was two inches taller than his father. "And if you turn me out and something happens to my brother, then where will your precious title fall? Ah, yes, to your brother." The comment caused the reaction he desired. His father took a step back and his face paled slightly.

"Two weeks," Richard said. "I ask for two weeks to consider your offer, my lord."

"What is there to consider?" Lady Catherine asked.

"The value of my life," Richard snarled. He moved toward the door, but his mother's hand on his arm forestalled him.

"Will I see you again?" Her eyes were filled with fear.

"At least once more," he murmured as he kissed her cheek before leaving the room and instructing that his things be readied for a journey.

~*~

Richard paused for a moment on the steps of Darcy House before lifting the knocker and allowing it to fall. Footmen waited at the carriage ready to divest the equipage of his belongings as soon as instructed to do so.

"The master and mistress have just arrived. If you will wait here a moment, I shall see if they are home to callers." Daniels held the door open for Richard to enter.

"I do not need to speak with them." Richard cast a glance over his shoulder to the carriage that waited on the street. "I need only to know if I can store my things here until I have a place where they can be sent."

Daniels raised an eyebrow slightly. "If you will wait, the master will see you directly."

Richard sighed. He had hoped that Daniels would simply allow him to leave his things and be gone. He had little desire to speak with anyone. He wandered into the sitting room and took a seat near the window where he could best appreciate the weak winter light before it faded to shadows.

He had only been seated for a moment when Darcy, followed by Elizabeth, entered the room with, what seemed to him, to be more haste than necessary. He sighed again and slowly rose to his feet.

"Why must you store your things at Darcy House?" Darcy asked, ignoring the normal pleasantries of greeting.

"I have nowhere else to put them at present," Richard replied. "I will send for them as soon as I have lodgings."

Darcy motioned to the chair from which Richard had just risen, and Richard obediently sat. It would do him no good to offend the cousin from whom he wished to obtain help.

Darcy unbuttoned his coat before sitting and leaning toward Richard. "The full story, if you will."

Richard scrubbed his face with his hands, settled back in his chair, and related the events that had led to his departure from home.

"Where will you stay?" asked Darcy.

"Not here," Richard replied, hearing the softness of his cousin's question, and knowing that it indicated Darcy's next comments would be to suggest that Richard stay at Darcy House. "It must be some place where my father cannot find me. I must be completely free from him for a fortnight." He blew out a breath. "And it must be what I could afford should I refuse his offer." He ran a hand through his hair. "I must see what my life will be and if I can abide it." He smiled wryly at Darcy. "So, you may not assist me aside from storing my things until I am able to keep them myself."

"Daniels has a sister who works for someone who rents rooms to respectable gentlemen."

Both Darcy and Richard looked at Elizabeth in surprise.

"I like to know about my servants' families," she explained. "We could ask him for the address, and if he knows whether there are any rooms available at this moment. If he does not, he may have recommendations." She smiled at Richard. "You are my family, and as such, I will care for you as far as you will allow me."

He ducked his head slightly, hoping to keep from her the effect that such comforting words had upon him. "I thank you, Mrs. Darcy."

"Elizabeth," she corrected. "Or Lizzy, if you prefer." She rose and gave his shoulder a soft pat. "I will inquire of Daniels while you men discuss whatever might remain to be discussed."

Richard dropped his head into his hands. "I cannot marry her, Darcy. I simply cannot."

"Because she is Anne? Or because your heart belongs to another?"

"Both," came the muffled reply.

Thankfully, Darcy leaned back in his chair and allowed Richard time to collect himself. After a few quiet moments, Richard drew his sleeve across his eyes before raising his head and smiling sheepishly at Darcy. It was rare that he shed tears in front of anyone, even Darcy, but his heart and his life were most likely damaged beyond repair.

"You shall stay the night." There was no question to Darcy's tone, and his countenance, though sympathetic, brooked no objections. "In the morning, you may visit whatever establishment Daniels tells us about, and then, if they are agreeable, you may take up residence there tomorrow or whatever day is mutually agreed upon." He leaned forward again. "You are always welcome here."

Richard nodded. He knew that neither of his cousins would ever turn him away. "But I must make my own way.

What kind of man lives on the charity of another when he is able-bodied?"

Darcy slapped Richard's knee. "Just know that I am here." He chuckled. "And if Elizabeth should discover that you have fallen into need and have not informed me, I shall leave it to you to explain yourself."

Chapter 3

THE NEXT MORNING, AFTER a less than restful night of sleep, Richard stood in front of number eight Bartlett's Buildings and checked the slip of paper in his hand once again to make sure he had arrived where he was supposed to be. It was a tidy little lane of houses, which were well-cared for and quite respectable looking. It seemed as if it would be a perfectly acceptable place to live. He raised his hand, rapped on the door, and waited. There was a shuffling inside, and then a friendly looking man with a quick smile and spectacles perched on the end of his nose opened the door.

"Come in. Come in," he said. "It is much too chilly today to be introducing oneself on the street. There is a hook on the wall for your coat and a table for your hat."

Richard thanked him and stepped inside. "I am Colonel Richard Fitzwilliam," he began. "I was given your address by my cousin's butler because he thought you might have a room to let?" He took a quick, sweeping glance around the hall where he stood. It, like the outside of the home, was tidy and well-cared-for. A few pictures and at least one mirror decorated the walls, and a worn, but clean, rug lay under his feet.

The man, who stood waiting for Richard to divest himself of his outerwear, chuckled. "My, my. I must be garnering a significant reputation if butlers are passing on my name." He motioned for Richard to follow him into a small sitting room off to the right. "Mrs. Wood, this is Colonel Fitzwilliam. Colonel, my wife."

Mrs. Wood put her stitching in her basket and rose to greet Richard. Her smile was as warm and ready as her husband's. She was at least six inches shorter than Mr. Woods and, at least, the same number of years younger.

"A pleasure to meet you, madam," Richard said with a bow.

"The pleasure is mine," she assured him as she returned to her seat and took up her work. "What brings you to our door on this cold January day?" She placed her feet on a foot warmer.

"The colonel said he is in need of accommodations." Mr. Wood motioned to a chair for Richard before taking a seat himself. "He says he was given my name by a butler." He turned to Richard. "Your cousin's butler, was it?"

"Yes. Mr. Daniels."

"Daniels is the butler or the cousin?" Mr. Wood was leaned back comfortably in his chair with his feet propped up on a stool, looking for all the world as if nothing was out of the ordinary and there was not a thing that could disquiet his repose. And yet, there was a liveliness of mind that could be seen in his expression.

"The butler."

"Oh!" Mrs. Wood placed her stitching on the table and became quite interested in the gentleman who had entered her house. "He must be Mrs. Letts's brother. I do believe she said her brother was Mr. Daniels, though she calls him Cyril more than Daniels, of course. Now, if my memory serves me as it should, I believe she said her brother works for Mr. Darcy, a rather wealthy and well-connected gentleman from Derbyshire. Is Mr. Darcy your cousin?"

Richard hesitated a moment before admitting the relationship.

"Oh, do not fear, Colonel; the cost of the room will not increase," she said with a grin. "The connection between you and Mr. Darcy only makes me most delighted to think you might take our room. It can be difficult to judge the quality of a tenant without knowing some of their connections. And Mr. Darcy's connections are good. Indeed, just his relations..." Her eyes grew wide. "Oh, my! Your family name is Fitzwilliam?"

"It is."

"Are you Lord Matlock's son?"

"For the moment, yes." He looked to Mr. Wood, who had yet to ask a single question of him. It appeared that the man preferred to let his wife take charge of the initial parts of the interview for possible new tenants. "I find that my father and I do not see things in the same way. I may only need the room for a fortnight, or I may need it for a much longer period of time."

Mr. Wood nodded thoughtfully. "Career choice or bride choice?"

"A bit of both, I am afraid. I would like to pursue a career in woodcraft and marry where I choose, but my father would see me marry an heiress and become either the manager of an estate or be perfectly idle."

"There is a duty in securing a title, I suppose." Mr. Wood cocked his head to the side. "Although I should think that is more your brother's responsibility than yours." He pulled his hands from his pockets and clapped them on the arm of his chair while lowering his feet from the stool at the same time.

"Come," he said as he rose. "I will show you the apartment, and we can discuss the particulars. I can see that my wife approves of you, and that's all I really need, other than assurance of prompt payment and such."

Richard followed him from the room.

"Has your father chosen a bride for you already?"

"He has."

Mr. Wood opened a door to the left of the hallway. "We dine here. There are two others besides you who live with us."

Richard popped his head into the dining room and looked around. It was well-furnished with a large table with eight chairs and a handsome sideboard along one wall.

Mr. Wood continued to open doors here and there and pointed to items that might interest Richard as he spoke. "My father may not have been an earl, but it sounds as if he was as set in his ways as yours is. Sent me packing when I refused to marry his partner's daughter, he did, and then, he gave my inheritance to my younger brother, who was willing to marry the girl." He chuckled wryly. "My brother was the reason I refused to marry her."

He stopped halfway up the second flight of stairs and turned to look at Richard. "He was in love with Fiona. It did not seem right to marry the lady my brother loved." He shrugged. "However, I would not have married her even if my brother had not been besotted with her, for I had already fallen in love with my Beatrice, and a man should not be separated from his love, even if it is costly." Again, he tipped his head to the side as he looked at Richard before continuing on up the stairs. "You've not already lost your heart, have you?"

"I may have." Oh, he had most certainly lost his heart. There was no *may* about it.

By this time, they had reached the top of the stairs, and Mr. Wood searched through his ring of keys as they walked to the end of the narrow hallway.

"If that is how things stand, you may stay with us for as long as you like, and should you find yourself able to offer for your lady love, I may be of assistance in finding an affordable living arrangement – one that is both comfortable and conducive to raising a family."

He pushed open the door to the room. "It is not large, but it is cozy – stays warm without too much need of a fire in the winter. The window allows for some breeze in the summer, but I'll not lie, it can be a bit stifling at times come July and August."

Mr. Wood was indeed correct; the apartment was cozy, both in atmosphere and size. There was a small sitting area with three chairs and a table pushed to one side, a bedroom with a bed, which looked comfortable enough, and a dressing room with a washstand and wardrobe. All in all, it was not grand nor elegant. However, it was adequate.

"I have a man," Richard said.

"Many do have a man or a maid – sometimes we have ladies as tenants, though currently, it is all gents. There is a place for your man in the servants' quarters, and he may dine with them. There is an extra charge, of course, to cover particulars." Mr. Wood motioned to the bell pull. "He will be the only one to answer, but a maid will be assigned to clean and collect laundry, and Mrs. Letts, our housekeeper, can be of assistance with whatever else you may need."

Richard turned a full circle and looked at the apartment once again. It was not what he was used to, but it was acceptable, comfortable even. He imagined he would feel at home here within a short time. He nodded and smiled at Mr. Wood. This was right. It was exactly what he needed. "If the price is agreeable, I will take it."

"Excellent." A smile split his face. He waved his arm toward the door, and Richard exited. "I have an agreement and your key in my study. You may take up residence as soon as I have your signature and money." He turned his key in the lock. "You mentioned that you like to work with wood. What kind of things do you make?"

"Boxes are my favourite, but I have also made some furniture." Richard replied as they descended the stairs.

"What kinds of boxes?"

"I have made a variety. My cousin has one in his study for his pen and ink, as well as a tray for collecting correspondence, and most recently, I designed a box for holding jewels for his wife."

Mr. Wood stopped short on the stairs. "I had forgotten that Mr. Darcy got married recently."

A cat that Richard had not seen until now brushed past his legs.

"That is Sally," Mr. Wood said. "She is a good cat, but she's known to upset a teacup now and then. In fact, she nearly caused a catastrophe last week when I was copying some papers." He had begun walking again and glanced over his shoulder. "I do some clerking for a solicitor," he explained.

Richard laughed and shook his head as he wondered what the odds were of this being the same cat which had delayed Rycroft's return to Netherfield. "Were they marriage papers, by any chance?"

"Aye, they were."

"For Lord Rycroft?" Richard asked.

"It is not for me to say," Mr. Wood replied.

"Of course, forgive me. It is just that my cousin was delayed by marriage papers that had to be recopied due to an unfortunate incident involving a cat and tea."

Mr. Wood chuckled. "I would not say that Sally is that particular cat, but I also would not say she is not. No matter where the truth lies in that," he scooped up Sally before opening the door to his study and then sat her back down and closed the door quickly, "she is no longer allowed in my study." He winked at Richard. "Especially when there is tea."

Chapter 4

"Was it acceptable?" Elizabeth asked as Richard was removing his hat and coat in the entry at Darcy House.

"It was. It is all very proper-looking, and Mr. and Mrs. Wood are very welcoming people. I felt at ease nearly from the moment I entered their home. Thank you, Daniels."

The butler only nodded in response, though there seemed to be a very pleased look in his eyes.

"You must tell me all about it." Elizabeth slipped her arm through his and led him to the sitting room. "I must be assured that you will indeed be comfortable and well-cared-for, and then, I believe our workshop has missed your presence." She tipped her head and looked up at him with a smile.

He could see why his cousin was so besotted with his wife. She was the very picture of everything bright and caring.

"I am certain the workshop would appreciate a visit from you as often as you would care to call on it," she added.

He chuckled as he took a seat near Darcy. "I shall do my best not to neglect it, but I do not wish to be anywhere my father might think to find me, for I have no desire to endure his arguments. I need to arrive at a conclusion on my own."

"I cannot promise that I will not give you my opinion." Darcy set aside his book.

Richard shook his head. "You do not need to share it. I am sure I can guess." Darcy believed in marrying for love, rather than advantage. He always had. But Darcy's life was far different from Richard's.

"Then, tell me, what is my opinion?"

Richard folded his arms across his chest and studied Darcy. "You think I should follow my heart as you have followed yours. However, I must remind you that my circumstances at present are somewhat less than yours have ever been." He held up a hand when Darcy opened his mouth. "No, I shall not hear of your assistance."

His cousin was a fine manager of all the monies that were in his domain, but he was by no means tight-fisted. Indeed, he was quite generous where there was need, most especially amongst those who were part of his intimate circle.

Darcy closed his mouth and scowled, causing Elizabeth to giggle lightly. "A gentleman's pride, wounded if given help and equally wounded if help is refused. You men are such strange creatures."

"They are strange indeed." Lady Sophia waved Daniels away before he could announce her as she entered the sitting room. "I pray you will pardon my intrusion, but I thought it best to leave my home for a while to give Rycroft and Mary some time to settle into the place." She rolled her eyes as if annoyed by the necessity of leaving her home. Her smile, however, let them all know just how delighted she was to have been inconvenienced to do so by the arrival of her newly married son and his wife.

She placed her hands over Georgiana's ears. "We shall not speak about the compromise," she warned. "Even if Rycroft has given me reason to believe that it was quite spectacular." Her eyes twinkled with amusement.

"That it was," Darcy agreed. "You know she will hear of it." He looked from his aunt to his sister.

Georgiana giggled and pushed her aunt's hands away from her ears. "Much to Mary's chagrin, I have been given a convincing demonstration."

Darcy's eyes narrowed as he looked at his aunt. "Then why place your hands on her ears?"

Lady Sophia shrugged. "It was merely my attempt at making you think I was doing my duty."

Darcy shook his head and chuckled as they all took their various seats. "While I am certain you do not condone such public displays of affection..." He paused to give his aunt a stern look.

"Oh, I do not."

If she had not been doing such a poor job of feigning a serious expression, Richard might have been willing to believe her. As it was, he was only reassured of what he already knew. Lady Sophia liked to skirt the edges of propriety at times.

"I am equally as certain," Darcy continued, "that you cannot help but be delighted with the results."

"Beyond delighted!" Their aunt cried.

Darcy gave his sister a stern look. "Not that the delight outweighs the wrongness of such actions."

Georgiana rolled her eyes as Richard had seen her do many times when her brother was belabouring a point that truly did not need as much attention as Darcy thought it did.

"You have all done an admiral job of instilling the rules of propriety and good sense in me, and experience has taught me caution in keeping them. You have nothing to fear from me. Besides," she said with a playful smile, "it was not Mary who created the scene. I believe the responsibility for that falls to our cousin with some help from you." She picked at a bit of something imaginary on her sleeve. "That is two compromises in which you have been involved, Fitzwilliam."

Darcy groaned while Richard chuckled softly.

"I still do not want you to be forced into a marriage." He took Elizabeth's hand. "Unless, of course, it is for the best and will result in your happiness." He held up a finger indicating he was not finished. "And has been sanctioned by me."

Richard laughed out loud. "Which, I dare say, will never happen as he is loath to allow you to grow up at all, let alone consider courtship and marriage."

"Very true," Lady Sophia agreed. "And that is understandable. However, whether he approves or not, your time will come when such things must be considered." She tapped her finger on her lip as she looked at Richard. "Of course, we shall have to remedy Richard's marital status first."

Richard tried to catch the grimace that such a statement provoked, but he was not fast enough.

"Ah, my brother." His aunt tilted her head to the side and nodded slowly. "He is a problem, and he is not pleased with my son's choice of bride. I have heard it."

"This morning," Georgiana inserted.

"Yes, before breakfast had concluded." Lady Sophia sighed. "He is wrong, of course. He always has been, but he has also always been too stubborn and foolish to see how wrong he is."

Darcy nudged Richard's foot with his own.

"I know," Richard hissed as he pulled his foot out of Darcy's range for tapping. But it did not matter if they all knew that his father was wrong. That would not change what his father did. It never had in the past. Why would it now? Lord Matlock did what Lord Matlock thought was best.

Lady Sophia arched one eyebrow. "Has something happened?"

Richard nodded. "I have a fortnight to choose either marriage to Anne or a significant, if not permanent, breach." Which meant, he would be cut off in all the ways his father could manage to cut him off. There would be no inheritance, and no recognition of him as son. Who knew if his mother would be allowed to see him or not? That was the part with which it was hardest to come to terms.

"Anne! Good heavens!" Lady Sophia could not contain her surprise. "You are staying here then?" It was not so much a question as it was a statement of the only logical thing to be done.

He shook his head. "I have signed an agreement to rent a room at the Bartlett Buildings."

Her brows furrowed.

"I do not wish for my father to be able to call on me, and I would like to see what my life might be like without..." He sighed. "Him."

"It is a respectable area."

Richard was not sure if his aunt truly thought that or was merely trying to support his decision. And then, much more quickly than he had imagined it would happen, her countenance changed from one of worry to one of restrained excitement.

"Two weeks?"

He nodded. A small amount of dread fluttered in his stomach at what might have her excited. He was sure that it included some sort of matchmaking scheme, and although he trusted her more than his father, he had no desire to be matched with anyone, save Kitty.

"Perfect," she said before turning to Georgiana. "Will you play for us?"

The change in conversation seemed to confuse Georgiana, but Richard knew that though the matter was no longer to be discussed, his aunt was not done thinking about it. Hoping to avoid any conversation that might include plans for his future, he rose and said, "As much as I would like to hear your talent, Georgiana, Elizabeth has promised me time in the workshop, and there is a small item I think my new landlord's wife would appreciate." He looked toward Darcy. "If you do not mind."

"My home is your home." Darcy rose and straightened his jacket. "I have a small matter that could use your expertise if you will allow me to accompany you?"

"I would welcome the company." He opened the door to the sitting room and waited for his cousin. From where he was, he watched Darcy gain his wife's attention before giving a tip of his head toward their aunt.

"I shall join you in the music room momentarily, my love."

Elizabeth smiled at him, one eyebrow raising and lowering quickly. "Some tea would be nice."

"I shall inform Mrs. Vernon," Darcy said.

"Will you join us?" Elizabeth asked Richard.

"If my project allows it."

"Have you met my sister, Kitty?" Richard heard Elizabeth ask his aunt as he closed the door.

"If Lady Sophia is scheming, and we all know she is," Darcy said, "she might as well be scheming in an appropriate direction."

"I appreciate the assistance."

"Do you?" Darcy asked with a laugh.

"In this, I do. But I do not want to live on the charity of a relation. Not even if that relation is you."

Darcy clasped his hands behind his back as he led the way to the workshop. "Are you opposed to my hiring your services?"

Apparently, today, it was not just their aunt who was scheming.

Chapter 5

RICHARD KNOCKED ON MR. WOOD'S study door and only pushed it open when he heard his knock acknowledged and after a quick look for Sally, who sat, swishing her tail and watching him from the far end of the hall. He slipped inside and closed the door quickly.

"I wanted to thank you for allowing me to read your paper." Richard placed the folded newspaper on the desk.

"A necessary luxury." Mr. Wood glanced up from his work. "A man likes to know what is happening in the world." He compared the paper beside him to the one in front of him, then neatly wrote one more word and returned his pen to its holder. "What are you about this afternoon, Colonel? A walk in the park or a visit to the museum?"

Richard laughed. "I shall be walking but not in the park. I had hoped to find some information regarding work that I might be able to do should my tenure at your residence become permanent. I spent yesterday assessing what my expenses would be. They are not above my current funds, even with the room I am renting, but if I intend to advance my place — and I do — I must find additional sources of income."

Mr. Wood rummaged through his drawer. "Ah, there they are."

He pulled out a stack of cards which he flipped through, occasionally stopping to pluck one out and put it to the side. Having exhausted his search of them, he picked up the small pile he had discarded and looked at them once again.

"None of these are too far from here. It should give you a start." He handed them to Richard. "Only one is a furniture maker, the others would do well to carry small boxes for various items in their shops. The jeweler, for instance, might be able to increase his clientele if he were to offer not only the jewels but also the boxes in which to keep them. And the dressmaker might like to have a box such as you gave to my wife for her pins and a larger one for her scissors." He shrugged. "Perhaps if a patron saw the items, they might request where they could get something so nice."

He drummed his fingers on the desk. "It might be of value to you to give a small box to at least one modiste and see what results you achieve." He lifted his pen from its holder as Richard thanked him and rose to leave. "Have you found a place to use as a workshop?"

Richard stopped with his hand on the door. "I have at least one possibility, but, for the present, Darcy has requested that I make use of his until I am better established."

Mr. Wood nodded. "A wise idea. I wish you well, Colonel."

Richard pulled the door open slowly and looked for Sally before slipping out and on his way to visit the places on the cards he held in his hand.

~*~

Kitty pressed a hand against the soft package she held on her lap and drew a deep breath before releasing it slowly.

"You will like Mrs. Smith," Mrs. Gardiner assured her.

"I am certain I will if you do." Her aunt had introduced her to Mrs. Havelston, and she liked Mrs. Havelston. She had also not met anyone yet today while calling with her aunt that she did not find to be lovely. Therefore, it stood to reason that any friend of her aunt was likely going to be someone Kitty would like.

"Then, what makes you sigh so?" A kind smile accompanied the question.

The answer to that question was not an easy one to make without tears, but Aunt Gardiner was proving to be all that Jane and Elizabeth had ever said she was – caring, gentle, wise, and so much more. Kitty most certainly could not refuse to answer in some way. So, she said it as simply as she could. "Giving up a dream." She shrugged and turned her face to the window as the Gardiners' carriage stopped in front of number eleven Bartlett's Buildings.

"Mrs. Smith will be happy to receive your linens for the baby, and I would not give up on your dream completely. At least, not yet."

On Jane's advice, Kitty had confided in her aunt about Colonel Fitzwilliam, which, as it turned out, had made asking her uncle to assist with payments from Mrs. Havelston much easier.

Mrs. Gardiner peeked out the window. "I see Mrs. Wood is on her way for a visit as well." She accepted the hand of the coachman to assist her from the carriage. "She will be most impressed with your work. She is quite talented with a needle herself, you know."

Kitty did not know. She had never met Mrs. Smith or Mrs. Wood or many of the other people Mrs. Gardiner had visited today. Of course, she had not often visited their aunt. It was usually Elizabeth or Jane who were requested. But with her three oldest sisters all married, she was next in line, and so her mother and her aunt had decided it would do her good to experience the city and help care for the young Gardiner children.

The baby linens that she was now clutching as she stood beside her aunt were ones she had made and kept in her locked trunk at the end of her bed. They were part of what she had hoped to take with her to her marriage. However, since she would likely never marry and knowing that she did not have time to make anything new for this visit, she had taken them out, for she simply could not visit a new mother such as Mrs. Smith without some item to give her.

"Mrs. Gardiner," the lady whom Kitty guessed was Mrs. Wood greeted as they all arrived in at Mrs. Smith's door at the same time, "it is a delight to see you. What has it been since we last were together?"

"At least a fortnight, I believe," Aunt Gardiner answered.

"How was the wedding breakfast?"

"It ended up that there were two weddings to celebrate."

"Indeed? Was the second a surprise affair?"

Aunt Gardiner chuckled. "To everyone, including the bride. Lord Rycroft managed to talk my niece Mary into marrying him without an ounce of preparation on her part."

The door to number eleven opened.

"She was married at the end of the ball I told you about."

"Oh, my! Married at such an hour?"

"Yes and celebrated the next day after Jane's wedding. She and her earl are returned to town now."

"That sounds like quite the exciting time," a lady who looked to be not older than Jane and whom Kitty assumed was Mrs. Smith said.

"Oh, it was, and that is why I have Kitty with me today instead of Mary as I thought I would have." Aunt Gardiner turned to Kitty. "This is my niece, Kitty. Kitty, this is Mrs. Wood and Mrs. Smith."

Kitty dipped a shallow curtsey. "It is a pleasure to meet you both. I have a gift for your baby." She extended her package to Mrs. Smith.

"What a wonderful surprise!" the lady cried. "I see you have your aunt's good heart."

"And you are such a pretty young lady, too," Mrs. Wood said.

"Thank you." Kitty took a step toward a small bassinette. "May I?" She had always loved children and often sought to spend time with them when Lydia would allow it.

"Oh, you must," Mrs. Wood encouraged.

Kitty took a seat near the bassinette and peered inside. Bright blue eyes blinked as they stared at the ceiling. Tiny feet poked at the blanket that covered them. Kitty sighed as the baby's fist found his mouth.

"He is sweet," she said to Mrs. Smith.

"Such a joy, he is," Mrs. Smith said. "I cannot believe how gracious the good Lord has been in giving Mr. Smith and me such a good boy." Her face beamed with pride as she stroked her son's head. "He looks a lot like his father, does he not, Mrs. Wood?"

"He is a fine image of Mr. Smith," Mrs. Wood agreed. "And if he grows to be half the man the reverend is, we will all be blessed." She was in the process of admiring the items that Kitty had brought. "I am sure I have never seen such fine work from one so young," she muttered.

Kitty blushed. "Thank you. I enjoy sewing."

"You have talent." Mrs. Wood laid the blanket to the side and ran her finger over the tiny flower buds that decorated the corner. "Very pretty."

Kitty thanked her once again and returned her attention to the baby.

"I saw you have a new tenant, Mrs. Wood," Mrs. Smith commented.

"Indeed, we do. I do not think we have ever had a better tenant – at least, not one with the connections he has, but it is not for me to share that. He is with us for at least two weeks, though my husband expects it might be longer." She lowered her voice to a whisper. "He has had a bit of a falling out with his father, but I will not say more than that. You know I am not given to gossip."

She turned to Mrs. Gardiner. "That was he who was just leaving when you arrived. A fine young man he is, very fine. Made me a beautiful box for my needles and thread. I met him one day, and he had the gift for me the next." She laughed. "And then, he apologized that he had not had time to engrave the top — as if I expected it to be decorated!"

Kitty kept her eyes on the baby, daring not to look up as her expression might lead to questions, and she did not wish to answer any questions regarding why such information would cause her eyes to fill with tears and her cheeks to grow rosy. It was silly, really, she told herself. There were surely many young men who could make boxes and engrave them. This could not be Colonel Fitzwilliam. He had a home and when he was not at it, he was with Mr. Darcy. She shook her head just a bit at her foolishness in imagining that he was so near.

Having gathered her thoughts into somewhat of an acceptable arrangement, she cooed at the baby, whose eyes had found her. "You are a very fine young man," she said as she gave his little toes a tap.

"That he is," agreed his mama.

Kitty accepted the cup of tea Mrs. Smith held out to her and took a biscuit from the tray. Then, settling back into her chair, she tried to focus on the conversation around her and not her thoughts of *him* until it was time to leave.

Chapter 6

UPON RETURNING FROM HIS calls that day, Richard collected the few items of post that had been delivered to his new address by one of Darcy's servants. It was as he had expected; his father had come that day to Darcy House in search of him.

I have not given him your location, his cousin wrote, *but I have told him that he might reach you by letter through me. It was the best I could think of to placate him. He said your mother was worried, so I attempted to reassure her through him that you were well-cared-for and were not living in some hovel or begging on the streets.*

He chuckled as he imagined the dramatics that his father had employed when pretending to be concerned for his son. His father being worried on his behalf was an extremely unlikely thing.

When questioned about what you were doing, I hope I have not overstepped my bounds in telling him that you are researching your options should you refuse his offer and be cut off. This did cause him to become very solemn and, if I am not mistaken, a bit shaken.

"He must be truly concerned that I will refuse," he said to the letter he held in his hand. "He is only shaken when he thinks his plans are to come to naught." The thought gave him a small amount of pleasure.

My wife sends her best and says to tell you that our workshop has been feeling neglected, and if it would help entice you to come for a visit, she will see to it that a tin of biscuits awaits you. I must warn you, however, that you will be expected to show yourself to her, so that she can see you are indeed well.

Do come soon.

F.D.

He would visit his cousin tomorrow, for he needed to make use of the workshop. Richard put the letter to the side and shuffled through the remaining post before checking his watch and readying himself for dinner.

"Good evening, Colonel, was your day a success?" Mr. Wood asked as they settled in for their dinner of stew and bread.

It was a meal that, according to Mrs. Wood, was a staple at number eight Bartlett's Buildings because it was economical, hearty, and easily held for those who were not available to eat at the prescribed time.

"It was. I must thank you once again for your assistance." Richard broke off a piece of his bread and spread a generous amount of butter on it. The meal might be basic, but it was delicious. The Woods' cook was among the best from what he had tasted so far in his short stay.

"The first jeweler was quite interested in my designs and has requested a sample of one. The furniture maker is not taking on new help at this time, but he has my information should he find he has need of assistance on any projects. I have decided to take your advice and have left visiting any modiste shops until I have a pin box to give them, so I will spend the whole of tomorrow, I imagine, in my cousin's workshop."

"Which modistes will you be visiting?" Mrs. Wood asked.

Richard made to reply but before he could, she had set her spoon down and clapped her hands in delight.

"Oh, you must start by visiting Mrs. Havelston. She is simply one of the best in town." She blushed and smiled. "I am a friend, so I might be a small bit partial, however."

Mr. Wood chortled at the comment, but his wife waved away any reply he might have felt compelled to make. "You know…" She leaned forward as if imparting a great secret. "One of her clients has recently become the new Lady Rycroft? It is true. Mrs. Gardiner was telling me just today — when I was visiting Mrs. Smith — about how her niece had recently married Lord Rycroft. It was quite the tale to be sure!" She took a sip from her wine glass.

"Mr. Gardiner, who is also a dear friend," she explained to Richard, "has always supplied Mrs. Havelston with the best quality materials, and her work is outstanding. You would be hard pressed to find better workmanship than what comes from her store. Do you have her card?"

Richard nodded. He had thought her name sounded familiar and so had considered visiting her first. Now, hearing Mrs. Havelston's name linked with that of Mrs. Gardiner, he remembered where he had heard it before. It was the name Kitty had mentioned when she told him that she had sold a design.

"And speaking of quality work." She lay a hand on her husband's arm. "You should see the things that Mrs. Smith received for the baby."

"I am sure I would not appreciate them as you do, my dear," her husband replied with a wink at Richard.

"Oh, to be sure you would not! But even you would be able to appreciate the care taken in their creation."

Mr. Wood sighed. "And would you care to tell me from whom these lovely gifts were received?"

"Oh, I would," she said with delight. "Mrs. Gardiner called, and she had one of her nieces with her. Such a lovely young woman and talented. With a heart of gold, I say, for she had made these things to lay by for when the need arose, and, hearing that she would be visiting Mrs. Smith — a stranger to her — she brought a gown, a cap, and a blanket." Her hand rested on her heart. "Oh, the delicate flowers that she had embroidered on the corner of the blanket." She sighed. "Lovely, just lovely."

Mr. Wood smiled at his wife and then looked toward Richard, whose spoon has stopped halfway to his mouth and was slowly lowering back to his bowl. "Is something amiss, Colonel?"

"Miss Katherine?" he whispered. It had to be her.

Mrs. Wood cocked her head to the side and studied him. "Her aunt called her Kitty. Do you know her?"

He nodded slowly.

Mr. Wood took his wife's hand. "I believe, my dear, that she is the one of whom his father would not approve."

Again, Richard nodded his response. "My cousin is Lord Rycroft," he said after a moment of silence. "And Miss Katherine's sister is his wife."

"Do you mean to tell me that your father does not approve of the new sister of an earl?" The incredulity in Mrs. Wood's voice made Richard's lips curl in a small smile.

"No more than he approves of the earl's wife or Mr. Darcy's wife." Richard sighed. "She is but a lowly gentleman's daughter in his mind. She has no connections and very little money, and is, therefore, unfit to be my wife."

Mrs. Wood huffed. "I thought my husband's father was foolish turning his son out for not accepting a wife when he loved another quite acceptable choice, but I see foolishness is not a respecter of class lines."

Richard chuckled. "Indeed, it is not." Foolish was a very good word for his father.

Mrs. Wood folded her hands in front of her and leaned toward him just a bit, almost as he imagined a mother might her child. "If you refuse your father's choice and chose this life — the life of a tradesman — will you offer for her?"

He wanted to. He truly wanted to, but could he? He shrugged. "She deserves more."

Mrs. Wood shook her head. "In my way of thinking, you are wrong about that. There is no more you or another could give her than for her to be loved completely. To be sure, servants and things make for a comfortable life, but is it a happy life when what you desire is the love of another?" She smiled at him and added, "Your stew grows cold."

Richard scooped up a spoonful of stew and put it in his mouth. Was there truly no more that anyone, even he, could do for Kitty other than to love her? Could he offer for her? He had already determined he would not marry

Anne, but in so deciding, he had thought to never marry, for how could he provide for Kitty and any children they might have on a tradesman's income?

Though his mind was deep in contemplation of Kitty and his future, he caught the name Mrs. Gardiner again in the Woods' conversation. He shook his head at his own faulty thinking. Mr. Gardiner was a tradesman, and his family did not suffer for it.

In fact, if Richard looked beyond his current situation to the world that surrounded him, he knew that there were many in trade who had families and many who had amassed great fortunes. How many times had his father complained about just that thing when speaking about Bingley?

He nearly laughed at himself as he realized that Bingley was a perfect example of what could be achieved through the dedicated work of a tradesman. He soaked up the remainder of his broth with the last bit of his bread. He savoured this last morsel as he sat back contentedly in his chair. Tomorrow, he would make a pin box and take it to Mrs. Havelston, and then he would call on the Gardiners. After all, he told himself, it was only polite to call on friends when one knew they were in town.

"Thank you," he said as he rose from the table, "for both the food and the conversation. It was exactly what I needed this evening. I cannot remember the last time that both my body and soul have felt quite so completely well-nourished." He was certain his heart had never felt this light before in his life.

"You are most welcome," Mrs. Wood said.

He turned to her husband. "I believe I will be staying indefinitely. No matter the cost, I cannot live with another when my heart belongs to Miss Katherine."

"Will you offer for her?" the man asked. "As I have said before, I can help you find suitable and affordable housing for a family."

The smile that curled Richard's lips started deep within him. "I believe I will. However, I will not marry her until I can provide for her better than I currently can."

"You will be a success. I know the sort who make their way quite well, and you are one of those people, Colonel," Mr. Wood assured him.

"I do hope you are correct. Again, I thank you for the meal and the words of wisdom." He sketched a shallow bow and with hope in his heart, took himself to his room.

Chapter 7

A DAMP, FRIGID GUST of wind made Richard draw his coat more tightly around his neck and duck his head so that his hat and not his face felt the greatest amount of sting from the coldness of the air as he hurried along the street. He had chosen to leave his horse and travel as most did – on foot. He hoped he would be able to keep his horse once he was cut off, but today, he was going to live as if he had no horse. His freedom was worth more than a horse, and for him, that was no small thing to say. He had loved riding from the first time he had been placed on the back of a pony.

"Pardon me," he said as he quickly stepped to the side, narrowly avoiding a collision with a footman who was assisting a lady to her carriage.

"Richard?"

He would know that voice anywhere. It was not just any lady who was returning to her carriage. He stopped and turned back. "Lady Matlock," he greeted his mother with a proper bow. "It is a pleasure to see you."

Her eyebrows rose. "Is it? I had thought you had forgotten about me entirely, since I have heard naught of you for four days."

He gave her a sad smile. "I apologize, but is that not that to which we must grow accustomed?"

She motioned toward the carriage. "Sit with me. Just for a moment. I shall not try to force you to return home with me, but the wind is biting, and it would be far more pleasant to speak if we were out of it."

He saw her shiver and knew he could not refuse her. "I will not tell you where I am staying or precisely how I have been keeping myself," he warned as he offered his hand to help her into the carriage.

"I believe I can tolerate my curiosity not being assuaged for a few minutes of your time, but it does mean that you shall, then, have to listen to me complain about your aunt."

She lifted her feet and put them on a warming box and then smoothed her skirts as Richard climbed into the carriage and took the seat across from her. It was nice to be out of the weather, and it was pleasant, in a bittersweet fashion, to be allowed to sit, perhaps for the final time, on this bench where he had so often sat in his life.

"*That* woman is truly lacking social grace!"

Richard chuckled and listened silently as his mother continued on for a few moments about the demands made on her staff by Lady Catherine and how Anne had spent the whole of her stay thus far in her chambers.

"I am convinced Anne is not at all as ill as she pretends."

Richard had often thought that as well – during nearly every visit he made to Rosings in the spring, truth be told.

"But, then," his mother continued, "I also cannot blame Anne for using the only means available to escape *that* woman. For that reason alone, I would like to see you marry her."

"Are you truly saying that I should marry Anne to save her from her mother?"

"It is not the most horrible of reasons to marry." Her eyes begged him to agree with her.

He shook his head. It was not the most horrible reason. Indeed, it was a far nobler reason than the one his father had presented, but it was still not an acceptable reason – at least, not for him. "She deserves to marry – and to be away from her mother – but I will not be the one to marry her, Mother."

She sighed, and concern etched a deep crevice between her eyebrows.

Richard drew a deep breath and took her hand. He had to tell her the truth of how things were and would be even if he had not reached the end of his two weeks of contemplation time. There was no one he wanted to marry except Miss Katherine Bennet.

"I have made my decision," he began and gave his mother's hand a squeeze when she sucked in a quick breath. "I wish with all my heart that I could marry Anne just so I could remain your son, but I cannot."

Lady Matlock placed her free hand on his cheek. The war of what she thought should be and what she wished for him played on her features. "You are certain?"

He nodded and turned his head to place a kiss on her gloved palm. "I am, and though I shall regret leaving you, I cannot bear to face the regret I would have if I stayed. I love her, Mother."

"More than me?" she asked softly.

He shrugged, unwilling to say the truth and cause his mother's pain, but equally unwilling to say he loved anyone more than he loved Kitty. "With all that I am and have."

"Oh, my son." She stroked his cheek.

"I am sorry, Mother."

"As am I." She leaned forward and placed a kiss on his cheek. "Perhaps your father will relent," she said hopefully.

"You know, as well as I do, that he never relents."

"I must hope." Her lips trembled slightly as she attempted to smile at him.

And he would, too. He turned his head and placed another kiss in his mother's palm.

"I beg your pardon, my lady," her footman said upon opening the door and interrupting the intimate scene, "but there is someone who wishes to speak to you."

"I have to go." Richard moved toward the open door.

"Take care," she said as he climbed out of the coach.

"I shall," he reassured her before turning to leave, but he did not move further. For standing behind the footman, waiting to speak to his mother was Kitty. "Miss Katherine," he managed to say.

She curtseyed deeply. "Colonel Fitzwilliam, my lady." She kept her head bowed slightly as she extended a parcel to Lady Matlock, who had exited the carriage behind Richard. "You left this behind, my lady. I am happy to have found your carriage still here, as it has saved me the trip to your home."

"Miss Katherine, is it?" Lady Matlock looked from Kitty to Richard, who was struggling to look anywhere but at the lady he loved. One of his mother's eyebrows arched in question.

Richard gave her a small smile.

"If you wish, my lady, or Miss Bennet, if you prefer." Kitty lifted her eyes to meet his mother's.

"Tell me, Miss Katherine, do you draw?" she asked as she accepted the package from Kitty.

Kitty looked at her in some confusion. To her, it likely seemed a strange question, but to Richard it was not. His mother was verifying what she suspected. She had seen the picture Kitty had drawn for him.

"I do, my lady."

"I am always curious about the accomplishments of other ladies," his mother said with an air of nonchalance.

She was a practiced actress – one had to be to navigate the *ton* as successfully as she had for years.

"The museum affords great opportunities for sketching," she continued, "though I find I do not enjoy the pastime myself." She lifted the package that Kitty had given her. "However, this is an activity I find particularly enjoyable." She looked at Kitty expectantly, as if she was waiting for Kitty to inquire about what activity it was that she found enjoyable. However, she was to be disappointed, for Kitty did not ask.

"Then, I am doubly glad to have been able to return it to you. It is important that everyone has at least one activity in which they find pleasure." Her eyes darted to Richard for a moment before returning to hold his mother's gaze again.

Was she saying that on his behalf? The thought made his chest swell a trifle with pride at her courage and devotion.

How could he ever consider anyone but her as his future? He could not. He would not.

"Indeed." His mother's lips tipped up as if she was pleased by Kitty's response. "Mine is embroidery," she said, answering the question that had not been asked as she lifted the package again. "This is thread for that purpose."

Kitty smiled, and not just politely. It was an expression that radiated her delight at what his mother had said. "I would not like to lose something so precious."

This time, his mother's lips did not just tip up as they had before. This time, they curled into an easy, relaxed, and utterly satisfied smile. He had known his mother would be charmed by Kitty.

"Do you enjoy embroidery?" she asked.

"Very much, my lady. I also enjoy a bit of millinery work, as well as sewing, but please do not ask me to play or sing, for I am afraid those are not among my talents." She pressed her lips together as if stopping herself from speaking and dipped a curtsey. "My aunt is waiting; I must return to her."

"Of course," Lady Matlock said. "Thank you for returning my package to me."

"I am happy to have been of service." She dipped another curtsey, and her eyes turned to Richard for a moment before she returned to the shop.

His mother placed a hand on his arm, and when Kitty had gone back into the shop, said, "You were right. I like her very much, and I can see why you do, too. She is sweet." Then, she entered her carriage and was gone, leaving Richard standing in front of Mrs. Havelston's shop and wondering if he should enter.

Chapter 8

KITTY CLOSED THE DOOR to Mrs. Havelston's dress shop and took a lingering look at Richard through the window. She had not known when she had volunteered to run the package out to the carriage that stood before the shop that the lady whom she was seeking was Lady Matlock. Nor had she expected to see him. She was glad she had even if she had not been able to speak to him.

"Was she still there?" Mrs. Havelston asked, coming from the back of the store.

"She was, and she was most appreciative to have the parcel returned." Kitty slipped off her gloves and bonnet before removing her wrap.

"She liked your drawing, my dear. I am not allowed to make that design, nor am I to show it to anyone, until she has first had a chance to wear it." Mrs. Havelston chuckled. "She paid me well for the privilege, and so I will pass on some of the proceeds to you." She placed her book of patterns back on the counter and returned her measuring tape to the drawer. "I told her I was working with a new designer, and she has made me agree that she is to have the first pick of the new work." She smiled and took Kitty's wrap. "Again, it is a service for which she is willing to pay handsomely."

"I did not know you made dresses for Lady Matlock," Kitty said.

"Oh, yes, I have for a few years now, and when she wears a particular gown that suits her, I often get a few new orders for the same dress in various fashionable colours and fabrics." She raised her brows and smirked. "Not that all the ladies should be wearing the styles that suit Lady Matlock. She is petite with delicate features, so what looks good on her does not look good on those who are... not petite, shall we say?"

Kitty chuckled. She had seen many young ladies follow what they thought was fashionable without a thought about how those style would actually look on them. She took a packet of papers from her aunt, who had offered to hold them while Kitty took the forgotten parcel to Lady Matlock, and handed it to Mrs. Havelston.

"These are my new drawings. Would you like any of them?"

Mrs. Havelston took the packet and began looking through the sketches. "Ah, these are lovely," she said. "And having seen Lady Matlock, would you not agree that they would be perfection on her?" She looked over her glasses at Kitty, who nodded her agreement. "As they would on you. You are very similar in size, I believe." She pursed her lips and frowned. "You are not so tall as she, nor do you bear the results of bearing children, but your features and structure are alike. I would like to make one of your creations for you if you would allow it."

"But you have an agreement with Lady Matlock."

Mrs. Havelston wrinkled her nose in displeasure. "That I do. Perhaps after she has had a chance to wear one?"

Kitty smiled. "Perhaps."

Mrs. Havelston placed the packet of papers under the counter. "Do you wish for me to give you the payment?"

Kitty shook her head as she heard the door open behind her. "We shall proceed as previously discussed." Her eyes must have registered her concern, for Mrs. Havelston only smiled and nodded in response before turning her attention to the newcomer.

"May I be of assistance?" she asked whoever had entered.

"I would like to take a look at your patterns and a sample of your work."

Kitty groaned silently at the sound of Miss Bingley's voice. She had hoped today would be a pleasant excursion, but it appeared it would be one taxing experience after another. It had taken a great deal of determination to greet and speak to Lady Matlock without betraying any particular fondness for her son. Now, she was going to have to endure at least a few words with Caroline Bingley.

No matter how pleasant Kitty tried to be to Miss Bingley, she was always greeted with indifference, if she was so fortunate, or disdain and ridicule, if she was not. She sighed and pasted what she hoped was a pleasant smile on her lips before turning around.

Kitty's smile faltered for one moment as she turned and saw that not only had Miss Bingley entered, but she had done so on the arm of Colonel Fitzwilliam. Although it was only a momentary falter, it was long enough for Miss Bingley to notice and to cause her to smile with satisfaction.

"Miss Kitty," she cooed. It was a grating sound that made the hairs on the back of Kitty's neck stand on end. "It is such a delight to see you." She raised an eyebrow, and her smile grew just a bit. It was obvious to Kitty that she was taking pleasure in the possibility of making her uneasy.

"And you," Kitty replied. "I trust Mr. and Mrs. Hurst are well?"

"Very well, I thank you."

Kitty shifted her eyes to Richard and bit the inside of her cheek to keep from laughing, for the look on his face was the complete opposite of Miss Bingley's. "Colonel Fitzwilliam, I trust you are also well?"

He smiled at her. "I am." He turned to Miss Bingley. "If you will excuse me, I shall not be of any use in looking at patterns and samples." He lifted her hand from his arm. "However, Mrs. Havelston, I would like to speak with you when you have finished with these young ladies. I would not wish to be the cause of their delay in proceeding on to whatever calls they may still have to make."

Caroline's countenance darkened as she looked first at Colonel Fitzwilliam and then Kitty before turning to her friends and Mrs. Havelston.

"I had no idea Lady Matlock frequented your shop," one of Miss Bingley's friends was saying. "Her gowns are delightful."

Kitty smiled as she watched Mrs. Havelston flip open the book of patterns to dresses she thought would suit the ladies before her and then send her assistant scurrying to retrieve three pieces of fabric.

Richard drew Kitty off to the side. "I told them my mother ordered dresses from here. It was the only thing

I could think of for why I was standing in front of the modiste shop, staring at the door."

Mrs. Gardiner joined them. "Was there some other reason for it?"

He lowered his voice. "I have a sample of a pin box to give to Mrs. Havelston. My landlord, Mr. Wood, suggested I give a few boxes to various merchants in hopes of creating a demand for my work." He pulled the small box out of the pocket of his greatcoat.

"It is beautiful," Mrs. Gardiner said.

"You are selling your work?" Kitty whispered with a cautious look toward Miss Bingley, whose attention was obviously not fully on what Mrs. Havelston was saying, as her eyes were on Richard.

"I am. There is an explanation for it, of course, but I fear it would be best not to discuss it here." He took the box back from Mrs. Gardiner. "May I call on you tomorrow?"

"Unless you prefer to dine with us this evening," Mrs. Gardiner replied. "We are always delighted to add to our numbers around the table."

"It would be a pleasure," he replied. "I will need the directions and time."

Mrs. Gardiner walked behind the counter and pulled paper and pen from the shelf beneath it.

Miss Bingley gasped slightly at the action.

"Think nothing of it, ma'am," Mrs. Havelston assured her. "Mrs. Gardiner and I have been friends these many years. She is welcome to use whatever she needs."

"Years?" Caroline tone was one of great interest.

"For nearly as long as I have been in town," Mrs. Gardiner said with a smile. She turned her attention to writing down the information Richard needed. As she tucked the supplies back onto the shelf, she bumped Kitty's drawings and sent them scattering on the floor behind the counter.

"Oh," one of Miss Bingley's friends said, "some of those are very nice."

"I am sorry," Mrs. Havelston said, "those are exclusive designs for a particular patron. They are not for general orders just yet."

Kitty's breath caught in her chest when she saw the drawings lying on the floor. She was almost certain that there was nothing on them to connect them to her, but still, she feared that somehow the connection might be made. Her eyes darted to the three ladies who were standing, watching Mrs. Gardiner gathering the sketches.

"Did you draw them yourself?" Caroline turned her attention back to Mrs. Havelston.

"No, but I shall be creating the patterns based on the sketches." She nodded to Mrs. Gardiner and Kitty, who were preparing to leave, then continued her conversation with Miss Bingley about how fortunate she was to occasionally find talented artists willing to share their work with her. "What lady does not wish to have a unique design with which to catch the attention of the other ladies and perhaps a gentleman or two when they arrive at a soiree?"

Kitty could not help but chuckle to herself as she heard Caroline's friends start to chatter about gentlemen and this hideous dress or that divine creation.

~*~

"May I see you out?" Richard looked to Mrs. Gardiner imploringly. He had no desire to be held captive in this shop with Caroline and her friends for any longer than was necessary. He would not have entered with them if they had not found him out front staring at the door like a besotted fool.

"Of course, you may, sir." She took his proffered arm and allowed him to escort her out of the shop.

"How long do you think they will be?" He glanced back at the shop.

"At least another quarter hour," Mrs. Gardiner said. "I would be surprised if they do not leave with an appointment to have an order fitted. Mrs. Havelston is a fine saleswoman."

Richard pulled out his watch to mark the time. "Is your carriage near?"

"Just over there." Kitty motioned down the street and then, taking the arm he offered, allowed him to lead her to the carriage and hand both her and her aunt into it.

Richard closed the door and watched as the carriage moved into traffic. He pulled out his watch, looked at the time once again, and pondered what he would do with the remaining time before returning to Mrs. Havelston's shop. The wind tugged at his hat, and he put a hand up to keep it in place. He sighed resignedly, it would be best if he just waited in the shop instead of skulking about on the street and in the cold.

"She's a pretty thing." A man stepped out of the shadows. "I suppose my brother is not fond of such a low connection." The friendly stranger, who was actually no stranger at all, put an arm around Richard's shoulder. They were evenly matched for size. Both were of slightly more than average height with a muscular frame. Of course, the man from the shadows, also known as Admiral Reginald Fitzwilliam, younger brother of Lord Matlock, was older than Richard by at least twenty years.

"No, he is not." Richard shook his head. "You always could find me, even when I did not wish to be found."

The admiral shrugged. "There are very few places I have not tried in an attempt to rid myself of my father and yours." He chuckled. "The sea was the best. Neither of them would step foot on board one of my ships. It was one of the best things about being in the navy."

Richard laughed. "I thought the women in foreign ports were the best."

His uncle clapped him on the shoulder. "I said one of the best, not *the* best. Now, what has you shuffling about this district? Buying a dress for a ball?"

Again, Richard laughed. He had always enjoyed his uncle's company, not that he often had the opportunity to see him as his uncle and his father were rarely on speaking terms. "I am researching the option of becoming a tradesman." He pulled the box from his pocket.

His uncle took it and turned it over in his hands. "For pins?"

Richard nodded.

"And would I be correct that your father is the cause of your foray into trade?"

"He is. I have until the end of next week to tell him that I am not going to marry his choice. I expect I will be in need of employment shortly thereafter, as my term in the militia is nearly at an end."

His uncle made a clucking sound as he handed the box back to Richard. "Well, as I said, she is a pretty thing."

"That she is," Richard said with a smile.

His uncle made a sweeping motion with his arm, indicating that they should begin walking. "You can tell me about her while you wait to see my friend Julie, Mrs.

Havelston." He shrugged. "I was not as brave as you. I married the sea instead of my father's choice or defying him to marry the woman I loved."

The comment made Richard's left brow arch in interest and question.

"Tell me about your lady first," his uncle replied, "and then when we have time, I will tell you about mine."

Chapter 9

SOMETIME LATER THAT DAY, after the sun was gone and the darkness of night had fallen, Richard stood before the Gardiners' home, waiting to be allowed entry. He did not wait long, for the door was opened nearly before the sound of his knock had faded. Giving his name along with his hat and coat to the servant who greeted him, he again waited, this time in the hall, to be introduced. He took note of his surroundings with an eager eye. This was the home of a well-to-do merchant, and as such, it was the sort of living arrangements he might hope to one day have for himself. It was not Matlock House or even Darcy House, but it was lovely and felt comfortable and welcoming.

"Colonel Fitzwilliam, it is a pleasure to see you, sir. A pleasure." Mr. Gardiner greeted him with a firm handshake and motioned for him to have a seat. "Dinner will be served shortly. May I offer you a drink while you wait? A bit of wine perhaps?"

The man stood beside a dresser that held several bottles of wine and a few glasses. This, too, spoke to Mr. Gardiner's success in business.

"My husband prides himself on his wine selections, Colonel," Mrs. Gardiner said with a laugh. "It would do you well to enjoy it."

"Then I will happily drink whatever you select for me." Richard took a seat near Kitty, who smiled and gave him a brief greeting. He barely refrained from sighing as he settled into the chair next to her. It was heaven to be near her. There was no way he would give this up for any inducement. He would work as long and hard as necessary to be here.

"My wife and niece tell me that you are thinking of stepping down from the first circles of society to join my realm." Mr. Gardiner handed Richard a glass of wine. "I shall refill it for your supper. There is no need to sip like a lady, so to speak," he said with a wink.

Richard took the glass and after a hearty sip began his explanation of his change in position. "My father is very set in the traditional ways of the aristocracy. I am not, and the difference in our opinions seems destined to lead to a parting of ways." Richard lifted his glass. "This is excellent, by the way."

"Thank you. I do try to only stock the best." Mr. Gardiner extended his legs out in front of him and crossed one foot over the other. "I suppose if your plans do not result in a parting of ways between you and your father, it will, at least, bring a lowering of your status through the removal of your inheritance or strictures being placed upon that inheritance."

"Precisely. Though I expect it to be a parting." And an ugly break it would be. It had crossed his mind that he might have to relocate to another city to make his life, depending on how punishing his father decided to be. Of course, Darcy had connections that could be used to sway his father into being merely harsh rather than crushingly cruel.

"It is a shame that parents can be so demanding." Gardiner sighed. "And it is not just in the highest circles that it happens. Bennet faced the same from his father."

"Papa?" Kitty asked in surprise. Apparently, this was a new story to her, just as it was to Richard.

"Aye, your father's father, your grandfather, did not approve of your mother since her father was from trade, and, according to him, any true gentleman does not have ties to trade."

Richard chuckled bitterly at that. "I have heard my father say nearly the same words."

"It is so wrong," Mrs. Gardiner said softly.

"Indeed," her husband replied. "And Bennet thought so, too, and would not hear of breaking off his relationship with your mother, Kitty, and so, the entail on Longbourn was created."

"I did not know that," said Kitty. "I thought it had just always been entailed."

Her uncle shook his head. "No, the entail is a recent thing. It was not a complete removal of your father as heir – your grandfather hated his cousin too much to cut your father off completely. Instead, your grandfather gave your papa a choice, and he chose your mother over an unfettered inheritance." Mr. Gardiner turned back to Richard. "I assume your father wishes you to marry well."

Richard nodded. "That is what he says, although again, our opinions on what that means differ. And so, he has selected a bride for me." He heard Kitty's soft intake of air, but he dared not look at her. "I have until the end of next week to accept or refuse his choice."

"And you are considering refusing?" Mr. Gardiner asked the question of Richard. However, his eyes were on his niece, and concern etched his features. He must know the extent of the wishes that he and Kitty had to be together.

"I am not considering refusing him, sir. I am determined to refuse him."

Mr. Gardiner's eyes shifted back to Richard, and a smile replaced his look of worry. "Am I to assume there is a reason of the feminine variety for this determination?"

As if the man did not know! "There is."

"Well, then." Mr. Gardiner rose to lead them into dinner, and Richard and the ladies followed suit, "we shall have to discuss your plans for your business. I am well-established and would do whatever is needed to assist you if it means the happiness of my niece."

"I beg your pardon, sir?" Had Mr. Gardiner just hinted that he expected a marriage between Richard and Kitty to take place even though Richard had not yet put his offer forward?

"Bennet has told me not to refuse you," Mr. Gardiner said. "I am correct to assume that my niece is your choice, am I not? I assure you it is not an assumption that is based on ignorance, and from what I have seen of you, Colonel, I agree with Bennet. You would make our Kitty a fine husband. That is, you would if she was your choice?" His tone lifted turning the statement into a question.

Richard felt his cheeks grow warm. This was not how he had anticipated the evening to progress. He had expected to discuss his business with Mr. Gardiner over their meal, and then he would discuss Kitty after the meal when they were alone in Mr. Gardiner's study. However, it seemed they had skipped the meal and the solitude of Mr. Gardiner's study and had jumped directly to Richard's offer.

With all eyes turned toward him and his heart beating wildly, he nodded. "You are correct. I would very much like to marry Miss Katherine if she will have me." As he spoke, he felt a small hand slip into his.

Mr. Gardiner smiled at him, nodding to where Kitty stood next to Richard with her hand in his. "I believe you have your answer." He turned to his wife. "We could hold the meal for a few minutes, could we not?"

"At least five," she replied as she followed him out of the room and closed the door.

Richard looked at the door for a moment as he gathered his thoughts before he turned to Kitty. He had prepared a speech before he had left home this evening, but it seemed to have gotten lost on the way to this moment. "I am not romantic —"

"I know." Kitty lifted his hand and brushed her lips against his knuckles.

That did nothing to clear his addled mind. Indeed, it scrambled it further.

"A simple question is all that is required," Kitty prompted.

"But, what about the pretty words that all women wish to hear?"

She shook her head. "I do not need them. I see your love for me in your eyes and the things you do. You have chosen me ahead of family and fortune. There is no need to put it into words."

"I would choose you before I would choose myself." He placed a hand, which had been made rough from working with his men in the militia and the wood he loved, on her cheek. "I do not have the means just yet to support a family," he began.

"But you will." She squeezed the one hand of his that she still held tightly.

He smiled and nodded. He had already known that he would be successful, for the prize he sought was the most precious that could ever be claimed. However, in this moment, he would gladly face whatever trials might come as he established himself as a tradesman twice over just to have her continue to look at him as she did now with such confidence in his abilities. "Yes, I will, and when I do, I would very much like to create that family with you. Will you marry me when I am established?"

A smile lit her face and eyes. "I would like nothing better."

"It will not be a life of ease," he cautioned. For a moment, despite his desire to have her as his wife, he doubted whether he was doing the right thing in asking her to share such a life. His thumb caressed her cheek. "You deserve so much more."

"I love you." She pressed her cheek more firmly against his hand. "I will be happy nowhere else, save at your side."

He knew that he felt the same. It was why he was prepared to defy his father. No matter the money and property he would lose by choosing her, he knew his life would never be so pleasant with those things as it would be with her at his side. Still, he could not resist asking, "You are certain?"

"Yes."

"Then, may I — "

"Yes. You must kiss me."

And he did — soft as a butterfly landing on a delicate flower in a garden, for she was so precious, so treasured. But even though it was a brief, gentle kiss, the emotion that passed to her through it and returned to him as she wrapped her arms firmly around him, pulling him close so that her head could lay on his heart was anything but gentle. It felt strong and unbreakable, and he indulged himself in storing up this feeling until a soft knock at the door drew them apart and sent them on to dinner.

Chapter 10

RICHARD WHISTLED TO HIMSELF as he descended the stairs Monday morning. His time over the past two days with the Gardiners had been extremely pleasant. He and Mr. Gardiner had discussed some possibilities for his business, and he felt encouraged having the support and guidance of a merchant who was so well-established. His smile increased as he remembered the few minutes of privacy that the Gardiners had allowed him with Kitty before he had returned home each time. He poured himself some coffee, and giving a greeting to Mr. Wood, settled into his seat and began to eat. They both ate in silence. Mr. Wood read the paper while Richard contemplated the events of the past two days and the things he planned to accomplish today.

"Oh, my," Mr. Wood said in alarm. "Oh, my." He lowered the paper and looked at Richard, who was just finishing his meal. "You will want to see this. No, no, that is not accurate. You do not want to see this, but you need to." He rose, folding the newspaper as he walked toward Richard. He clapped Richard on the shoulder as he lay it before him. "I am grateful my father was not so scheming as yours." He pointed to the announcement of the engagement of Mr. Richard Fitzwilliam to Miss Anne de Bourgh.

Richard snatched the paper from the table. "No." He shook his head. He could not have read what he just read. His eyes skimmed the words on the page once more. He had read what he thought he had read. "No, it is not true! I am promised to Miss Katherine."

The room felt as if it were making circles around him, and he was aware of the sensation of his breakfast fighting to stay contained in his stomach. How could this have been printed? He still had a week before he had to tell his father of his decision. Unless —

"No, she would not." This simply could not be his mother's doing. She had promised.

He stood with the paper still grasped in his hand. He had to get to Kitty. She needed to know that this was not true. Rushing from the room, he grabbed his hat and coat from the chair near the front door and ran into Darcy as he stepped into the street.

Darcy took note of the paper in Richard's hand and the way his coat was thrown on but not fastened. "I see you have seen it." He placed a hand on Richard's arm. "Take a moment to think before you act."

Richard shook his head and pulled his arm away. "No. There is no time. When Katherine sees this..." His voice trailed off, and he closed his eyes as if it could prevent him from feeling the pain that he knew this announcement would bring to Kitty.

Darcy stepped in front of him. "She will be hurt, but a letter of explanation sent immediately might stem some of the damage."

Richard shook his head again. "She is not at Longbourn. She is in town." If only she were more removed from his father's manipulation. Anger swelled in him at the thought of his father's callousness. How dare he hurt Kitty like this! He would deal with his father later. Presently, he needed to go to Kathrine with all haste.

"With the Gardiners?"

Richard nodded. "I must go." He stepped around Darcy and ran down the street and around the corner just as a carriage was drawing to a stop before number eight Bartlett's Buildings.

Darcy had never seen his cousin in such a fit of agitation, and for a moment, as he watched him running down the street, Darcy considered chasing after him.

"I see I missed him," the new arrival said.

Turning to see who was speaking, Darcy's eyes grew large and his mouth opened just slightly before forming a pleased grin as he recognized his uncle, Admiral Fitzwilliam.

He chuckled at Darcy's expression. "Richard was just as surprised to see me on Saturday." He looked down the street in the direction Richard had taken. "I had hoped to ask him how his evening with his lady had gone. I did try to call on him yesterday, but he was out. I assumed, therefore, that I might be gaining another niece in the near future."

Before Darcy could question his uncle about his statements, Mr. Wood had joined them and was introducing himself.

"I can tell you what you wish to know," Mr. Wood said, "The colonel was successful. He asked his young lady to marry him and was accepted. He has not stopped grinning since that evening, and he was whistling his way into the day until he read that bit in the paper."

"He proposed to Kitty?" Darcy groaned and scrubbed his face.

"And was accepted," Mr. Wood said.

"That adds a wrinkle to this mess," Darcy muttered.

"What bit in the paper?" asked Admiral Fitzwilliam.

Darcy pulled a newspaper from his pocket and handed it to his uncle. He was allowing his uncle a moment to read the announcement when a horse carrying a finely dressed rider came up the road at a fast pace, then slowed, and finally stopped in front of them.

"Darcy, you are not easy to find." Rycroft swung down from his horse. "Uncle Reginald!" He embraced the man and thumped him firmly on the back. "My mother will be delighted to see you." He cocked his head to the side. "You are planning to call on her, are you not?"

"Of course." The admiral laughed. "I dare not slink back to the coast without seeing her."

"Mr. Wood." Rycroft nodded his greeting to the gentleman. "Now, why are we all here?" He folded his arms across his chest and waited for an explanation.

"Colonel Fitzwilliam is my tenant, my lord," Mr. Wood said.

Rycroft's brows rose. "Indeed?"

Darcy nodded. "While you have been otherwise occupied, our cousin's life has been crumbling apart."

"Crashed to the ground this morning," the admiral said.

"Perhaps you would like to use my sitting room for this discussion," Mr. Wood offered.

"Capital idea," the admiral said.

Rycroft led the way, stooping upon entering to scratch the ear of what he called a naughty cat.

"How do you know Mr. Wood so well?" Darcy asked.

"He works with my solicitor as a clerk," Rycroft answered. "Now," he took a seat, "the lovely Mrs. Darcy said that I would find you here and that you were in need of my assistance, Darcy."

"You spoke to my wife?"

Rycroft nodded. "I came to see if you would care to go for a ride, and she greeted me. It seemed most urgent that I find you, so I spared no time in coming here."

Darcy smirked slightly. Despite the seriousness of the matter at hand, he could not resist a small tease. "*Your* wife did not wish to ride with you?"

"She insists on spending time with my mother and *your* sister." He rolled his eyes. "I was instructed by all three that I was not needed for the morning."

Darcy laughed along with his uncle and Mr. Wood.

"Could we return to the subject of Richard?" Rycroft asked in a slightly irritated tone. "What has happened to cause him distress?"

"His father has demanded that Richard marry Anne."

Rycroft's jaw dropped open slightly. "Cousin Anne?"

"Yes," Darcy said. "But, he has decided he will not marry her."

"Which led him to my door in search of accommodations," Mr. Wood added.

Rycroft, with brows drawn together, nodded to each bit of new information as he took it in. "I assume that his father has threatened to cut him off if he does not comply and marry Anne?"

"Precisely," the admiral said. "It is a common tactic with the earls of Matlock, it seems."

Rycroft's head tipped as he gave his uncle a curious look, but instead of pursuing his uncle's comment, which had also piqued Darcy's interest, he asked, "But the breach has not yet occurred, has it?"

Darcy sighed. "Officially, no. But in reality, yes. Richard asked for two weeks to contemplate his future, but his father has not honoured that. The paper." He nodded to his uncle, who handed Rycroft the paper and pointed to the announcement.

Rycroft let out a long slow whistle. "So, Richard has little hope of escaping a marriage of convenience."

"It is worse than that," Darcy said. "You may not have noticed much other than Mary when in Hertfordshire, but our cousin has lost his heart to Kitty."

Rycroft blinked. "I knew there was an admiration on her part and a fondness on his, but has it truly progressed to this?"

Both Darcy and Admiral Fitzwilliam nodded.

"He proposed to her and was accepted evening before last," Mr. Wood said.

Rycroft sank back in his chair. "What do we do?"

That was the question. Lord Matlock would not simply retract his announcement, and they all knew it. Ideas were passed about, discussed, and discarded.

"There is always Gretna Green," Mr. Wood suggested.

"It is not an unworthy option," admitted the admiral, "but what I truly think we need is my sister's help." He looked at Rycroft. "Your mother has always been able to sway our brother. I do not know what she holds against him, but whatever it may be, it is effective. Perhaps it will help Richard out of this mess."

Darcy certainly hoped that Lady Sophia would hold the key to unlocking a happy resolution for Richard and Kitty. The sight of his cousin in such a state as he had been in this morning was not one that was easily forgotten.

"Very well," Rycroft said. "Then, I say we go talk to my mother, and, if that does not work, then we shall cart them off to Gretna Green at midnight." He stood. "I can well imagine Richard's state of mind, as it was not long ago that I was feeling as he is." He looked around the group. "Do we all convene at Rycroft Place, or should one of us go in search of him?"

"He was on foot and seemed to be headed to the merchant district. I would say he is at the Gardiners'," Darcy said. "He needs someone. I will go and bring him to Rycroft place as soon as possible."

"Bring Kitty, too," Rycroft said before turning to their uncle. "Well, Uncle, it seems you are due for a visit to my mother and to meet my wife." He smiled and threw an arm around his uncle's shoulders. "I must caution you that Mary can be a bit rules-minded."

His uncle chuckled as the party moved toward the door. "And she married you?"

"Fortunately, yes." He gave a nod to Mr. Wood. "Thank you, sir, for the use of your sitting room. We will hopefully return your tenant to you in good order." He back turned to the admiral. "I will ride on ahead and warn the ladies that their morning plans are about to be altered." He winked at his uncle. "There is no need for us all to get a lecture." He held up a finger. "But you must never tell Mary I said that. She thinks it shows her in a poor light."

His uncle raised a brow and shook his head. "Is there no hope for you?"

"Very little," said Rycroft with a laugh. "Truly, I do not say such things to just everyone. At least, not any longer."

His uncle groaned. "And she married you?"

"Fortunately, yes." Rycroft swung up onto his horse. "She is the loveliest lady in all of England, if not the world." He clucked to his horse and, with a wave, was off.

"If not the loveliest, at least, the most tolerant and forgiving," muttered his uncle with a shake of his head.

"Excessively forgiving," Darcy agreed with a chuckle. "And she is just what he needed."

"I look forward to meeting both your wives and seeing my other nephew as happily married." He gave Darcy a pointed look. "Go get him, Darcy. He is not going to be another Lord Matlock casualty. Tell him that."

"I will." Darcy wondered at that comment and the one his uncle had made earlier, but now was not the time to discover the story that lay behind them. Right now, his cousin needed him.

Chapter 11

"Miss Bennet."

Kitty stopped, drew a breath, and took a moment to affix a smile to her lips before turning toward Miss Bingley. "Good morning, Miss Bingley."

She looked past her to the two ladies who stood with her. They were the same two ladies who had been with her the other day. Perhaps if she looked at them, Miss Bingley would remember to introduce them to her, although if they were friends of Miss Bingley, perhaps it was better if she did not know who they were.

Miss Bingley caught the direction of Kitty's gaze and with a look that said she was being forced to do something quite disagreeable, she said, "Miss Ivison, Miss Pearce, this is Miss Bennet. She is the sister of my brother's wife."

"Another Bennet?" Miss Ivison cried. "There certainly are a lot of you."

Her comment made all three ladies titter, and Kitty was now certain she did not wish to know any of them. If only there were a polite way to turn and leave them.

"There are five," Miss Bingley said.

"Five?" Miss Ivison's voice dripped with disapproval. "Are you all so *daring* as Lady Rycroft or Mrs. Darcy?"

Kitty did not miss the particular emphasis placed on the word daring. "Not Mrs. Bingley," she replied with a smile. "And I do not think of myself as particularly daring, but I imagine Lydia does." She spoke in what she thought was a way very similar to Lydia when she was attempting to shock someone into leaving her alone.

"Yes. Well," Miss Bingley said with a cunning look and smile for her friends, "it seems *you* shall have to find a new beau."

"Pardon me? I do not understand your meaning."

"I am speaking about your beau, Colonel Fitzwilliam, being outside your grasp," Miss Bingley said with a flutter of her lashes. "It is in all the papers. Do you not read them?"

"I have not read it today."

"One should always read the society pages if one wishes to be current on all the important news." Miss Ivison made a show of shivering. It was not that cold out this morning, and she was dressed warmly from what Kitty could see. "We should hurry. We have an appointment, after all." Contrary to her words, she made no move to depart from Kitty's presence. "Were you also on your way to the modiste shop again today?"

"I am." A sense of dread began to settle in Kitty's stomach. It was obvious that these ladies were not about to leave her alone. For what purpose she did not know, but she suspected it was not a pleasant reason.

"Do you work there?" Miss Pearce, who had not spoken to this point, tipped her head and studied Kitty.

"No." The sense of dread began to blossom. "My aunt is there. She and Mrs. Havelston are good friends. I was just getting some trim for my bonnet from the milliner." She motioned toward the milliner's shop.

"Hmm," Miss Pearce said. "I thought perhaps you might assist her — recording measurements, gathering material... *drawing patterns*." She paused and raised a brow as if she knew something that Kitty did not before continuing. "Your mother is from trade, after all, so it must be in your blood."

Kitty was at a loss for how to respond to such a comment.

"Then, I say it is very good that the colonel is safe from her machinations." Miss Ivison gave a small gasp and covered her mouth as if surprised by a thought, but her eyes said she was actually amused and not in the least shocked, as she feigned. "Although, some men do keep mistresses."

Again, all three ladies tittered.

Outrage bubbled inside Kitty. How dare they insinuate that the colonel was so disreputable, or that she was without morals? She straightened her spine and silently drew a breath, tamping down her anger. "If you will excuse me," she said. "I find I have had enough of your insults."

She moved to leave, but Miss Bingley stopped her, putting an arm around Kitty's shoulders and pointing toward Mrs. Havelston's shop. "Look, there he is with his mother. I wonder if Lady Matlock is helping him purchase something particular for his bride."

"His bride?"

"Yes, Miss de Bourgh – his cousin, I believe?" She turned toward her friends who confirmed it.

"It is in all the papers, remember? Oh, no, I had forgotten you have not read it yet." She released Kitty and smiled smugly.

Dread had turned to horror. It could not be true. It just could not be. "If you will excuse me, I must go." Kitty blinked against the tears that threatened to spill from her eyes. It could not be true. It simply could not be, she repeated to herself as she walked as quickly as she could toward Mrs. Havelston's shop. He had promised to marry her. He could not be promised to another. He just could not be.

~*~

"Did you tell him?" Richard stepped between his mother and her carriage as she exited the modiste shop. He had been on his way to the Gardiners' when he saw his mother's carriage turning down this street. Likely the driver had been returning to collect her at the end of her appointment.

"Good morning." Lady Matlock attempted to step around him, but he would not allow it. "Have you forgotten all your manners after so few days living with the lower class?"

"It is not a good morning," he growled, "and I wish to know if you are responsible for it or not."

Lady Matlock waved away the footman who had stepped up next to her. "I have no idea of what you speak."

Richard's replying laugh was bitter and cold. "You know very well of what I am speaking. You do not go a day without checking to see who has been engaged to whom. It is nearly as important to you as your first cup of tea." He held the paper out to her. "After I spoke to you the other day, did you tell Father of my decision?"

She pushed the paper away. "I told no one of our meeting. No one." She tugged nervously at a glove. "I did not know that had been submitted until after it was done."

Richard turned from her and threw his hands in the air in disgust. "He could not give me even two weeks?"

"He knew you would not accept." She placed a hand on his back. "We all knew — " She stopped as she saw that they were drawing a crowd.

Richard did not care if the whole world knew his business at present. His life was already in ruins. A public disagreement with his mother would only make his father unhappy, for Richard could not be made any more unhappy than he was. And so, he was going to continue their discussion until he saw who the crowd included. Katherine. She had seen it. He could tell by the pain in her expression she had seen it.

"Is it true?" Kitty stopped in front of Richard. Her lips trembled, and she closed her eyes and tipping her head, gave it a little shake as if trying to clear it. She opened her eyes, and he saw pain and fear mingled in them. "Are you..." She swallowed and shook her head again as she pressed her trembling lips together. She was trying valiantly to keep from crying. "Are you promised to another?"

Richard placed a hand on her arm, but she drew away. He looked to his mother and then back at her. "I am not, but the papers say I am."

Kitty pulled her lips between her teeth and nodded as a tear slid down her cheek. "If it is in the paper," she said in a quiet trembling voice, "then it is as good as done."

"Katherine..."

She shook her head. "I will not hold you to your promise to me. You must do what is expected."

The tears flowed freely down her cheeks now, and it tore at Richard's heart.

"Is it not enough to cast your child aside?" She looked past Richard to Lady Matlock. "Must you also require he sacrifice his heart?"

She placed a hand on her chest, and visibility drew a breath as if it was a difficult thing to do. Then, she moved that same hand to Richard's arm. "You will always have mine." Her voice was no more than a whisper.

She withdrew her hand and stepped past him toward the shop. Her shoulders sagged as if she were being pressed down. She took one step away from him. Then, another. His hope of a happy future. Everything he held dear was walking away from him. She swayed. Her legs wobbled and –

"Katherine!" Richard shoved past his mother and caught her before she hit the ground but not before her head had made contact with the edge of the doorframe. He looked at Miss Bingley. "Hold the door." He barked out the command as if she were one of his recruits. And just as if she were one of his men, she jumped and did as she was instructed.

"We need cloth, Mrs. Havelston. Quickly." He had seen blood before, many times, but to see the trickle of blood running down Katherine's white face, made his stomach roil.

"You need to sit down, Colonel," Mrs. Gardiner said. "As soon as we have a dressing on her forehead, you may place her in my carriage. It is out front." Her voice was soft and soothing. Her touch on his arm as she led him to a chair was light.

"Oh, my, oh, my," Mrs. Havelston said as she brought some cloth over to where Richard sat with Kitty in his arms and placed it on Kitty's forehead. "She will need a stitch or two, to be sure," she said to Mrs. Gardiner. "What happened?"

His mother stepped forward. "She received some distressing news." She removed Richard's hat and ran her hand through his hair as she had when he was a child, and she was trying to soothe him. She handed the paper, which Richard had dropped, and she had obviously retrieved, to Mrs. Gardiner. "There seems to be a mistaken announcement."

Richard's brow furrowed and his eyes snapped toward her. A mistaken announcement? There was no mistake. It was purposeful – false, but intentionally published. She placed her hand on his shoulder and shrugged. "I am your mother." Her gaze flicked to Kitty. "She is right. I cannot ask you to sacrifice your heart."

"But Father…"

"We will see what can be done," she murmured. "I make no promises other than my support."

Chapter 12

RICHARD SHIFTED KITTY SLIGHTLY in his arms as Mrs. Havelston finished the job, which the door frame had started, of removing Kitty's bonnet. His mother's words were a balm to his wounded heart, but he knew that there was likely little she could do.

"Did she see the paper?" Mrs. Gardiner asked.

"I do not believe she did," Lady Matlock replied slowly as if she was trying to piece together what had happened. "She asked if it was true, but did not seem to know what was said in the paper."

"Then how did she hear?" Mrs. Gardiner tilted her head and looked at the three ladies who stood near the door.

"We have an appointment with Mrs. Havelston," Miss Ivison said.

"Oh, my, I cannot think to keep an appointment at a time like this. Miss Kitty is like family, you see." She looked behind her to her assistant. "Miss Mallory, would you be so kind as to take these ladies' measurements and record their selections? Perhaps one of them could write for you while you work with the others." She added another cloth to the wound on Kitty's forehead. "I would not ask it of my clients," she explained, "but it is the only way I will be able to keep your appointment. However, if you prefer another day, that can be arranged."

Miss Ivison huffed. "You would cancel an appointment for someone like her?"

Mrs. Havelston straightened and turn to face Miss Ivison. "I have already informed you that Miss Kitty is like family."

Miss Ivison shook her head and lifted her chin a bit higher. "She is nothing but a poor country miss who sells you drawings."

"I beg your pardon?" Mrs. Havelston's hands rested on her hips and her features were set in a grim expression of displeasure.

"There was a slip of paper in the pile which scattered the other day that had her name on it." Miss Ivison lifted her chin, a smug look of satisfaction on her face. "She is your new designer." Her tone was mocking. "A gentleman's daughter who has lowered herself to work in trade and hoped to persuade the son of an earl to marry her. I am surprised she did not affect a compromise as her sisters have done to snare their husbands."

If Richard were not holding Kitty, he would remove Miss Ivison from the store!

Mrs. Gardiner gasped and covered her mouth with her hand while Mrs. Havelston's eyes narrowed and with a slight flip of her head, turned away from Miss Ivison indicating they had nothing further about which to speak.

Next to him, Richard's mother inhaled sharply. She looked down at Kitty. "She is your designer?" Gently, she took one of Kitty's hands in hers and smiled softly at Richard. "I do not care if she is," she whispered.

"That I cannot say, my lady," Mrs. Havelston replied. "But what I can say is that these ladies, Miss Mallory, are never to have an appointment with me. Not today, not ever."

Miss Ivison laughed. "I would think twice before denying our business. My father and the fathers of my friends are men of means."

"Your money is not needed. Be on your way." Mrs. Havelston turned back to tending Kitty's wound, which had slowed its bleeding.

"Mrs. Havelston will always have *my* business, and I will continue to refer my friends. I dare say I have more sway than you. It will be too bad that you will not be able to wear any of the exclusive styles Mrs. Havelston creates for me. Of course, I am not sure you could carry them off, so perhaps that is to your benefit."

In that moment, Richard was sure he had never been so proud of his mother as she leveled her most contemptuous look at Miss Bingley and her friends.

With a huff, Miss Ivison, Miss Pearce, and Miss Bingley turned to leave just as the door opened, and Darcy stepped into the shop.

"Hold the door, sir," Mrs. Havelston said. "Colonel, if you will?" She motioned for Richard to carry Kitty out of the shop. "We had best be getting this young lady to her aunt's house."

Kitty groaned and her eyes fluttered open for a moment when Richard stood. "Shh," he said, kissing her gently on the forehead. "All will be well," he whispered. "I have you."

He held her more firmly as he carried her to the carriage and wished with all his heart that his words were actually true. But how could they be? Then, when the carriage door was opened and with a sigh of regret and another kiss to her forehead, he placed her gently next to her aunt. His shoulders sagged as he watched the vehicle move slowly down the road.

"Such theatrics," Miss Ivison said as she passed him, "Swooning over a bit of news. Indeed!"

"Not unlike her sisters in her attempts to find herself in some gentleman's arms," Miss Bingley said.

Richard's hands clenched at his side as he spun toward them. They were utter idiots!

"You boorish, babbling harpies! If Miss Bennet does not recover, I shall personally see to your ruin."

He stepped closer and lowered his voice to a growl. "I promise that there shall not be a place left in polite society which will accept you." He began to turn away, but thought better of it, and added, "And should I hear that you were the cause of her distress, I may ruin you anyway. Therefore, I would advise you to take the first offer of marriage you receive — if you receive any — for it may be your last."

Miss Ivison was, of course, the first to find her voice. "Colonel," she began in a saccharine tone.

"Do. Not." He fixed a glare on her that he knew had frightened many a young officer in his command. "You are no longer welcome to speak to me, and I most certainly do not wish to speak to you." He turned and walked away, leaving the three ladies red-faced with their mouths hanging open. He would have walked right past his cousin and his mother had Darcy not stopped him.

"What happened?" Darcy asked.

"I cannot speak of it just yet. I need to expend some energy, or we shall both suffer from my current state of mind."

Darcy's eyes searched his for a moment before his cousin gave a nod of acceptance. "We are meeting at Rycroft Place."

Richard nodded. "I will be there."

"As soon as possible?"

Again, Richard nodded.

"Are you going to walk the distance?" his mother said. "The wind is cold."

He shrugged. "I may see if I can get a hack along the way."

She sighed. "Where do you board? I can have my carriage meet you there."

He shook his head. "I do not wish for you or anyone my father employs to know."

"I will not tell your father where you are," she said in exasperation.

"It is best if you do not need to keep it from him," Richard said softly. He was already going to be the cause of discord between his parents. He did not need the secret of where he was living to be the reason his mother found her life unbearable.

"Darcy." She turned to him with a look that implored him to do something.

"I know where it is. I will meet you there, Richard."

"Thank you," Lady Matlock said. "I am not as evil as you all might think."

"I do not think you are evil," Richard assured her. "You are too bound by society and my father, but you are not evil."

He turned away and then back. "It was my knowing how good your heart is that made my decision so difficult. It is why I have tolerated my father's demands for as long as I have. I know what you expect of your sons, and I have no desire to disappoint you. That being said, I cannot do what he asks. I simply cannot." He closed his eyes and shook his head. "And now, I do not know how to avoid it."

In all honesty, he wished to sink to the ground and hold his head in his hands. He knew that to break an engagement, whether he had willingly entered it or been duped into it, was no small matter and would not be tolerated by either his father or Lady Catherine. There would be penalties which would have to be paid, penalties which were, no doubt, calculated to make his breaking the engagement an impossibility.

"That is why we are meeting," Darcy said to Richard, with a sidelong glance at Richard's mother. "There must be something that can be done."

Richard shook his head. He wanted to believe there was something, but he knew his father.

"Do I wish to know who is included in this we?" his mother asked.

"Rycroft and his wife, myself and my wife, Lady Sophia, Admiral Fitzwilliam, and Richard."

Lady Matlock's brows rose as he listed the names of Lord Matlock's brother and sister. "So nearly the whole family is against my husband?"

"That is all for the present." There was a steeliness to Darcy's tone.

"There will be more?" Her hand flew to her chest and her eyes grew large.

Richard turned to leave but hesitated. Did it really matter how many more were on his side? Would any of it sway his father?

"Go," Darcy said. "I will come get you."

Richard sketched a shallow bow to his mother and began his walk back to his home at Bartlett's Buildings as Darcy answered his mother's question.

"I may not have a title, Aunt, but I am not without my sphere of influence. I do not know how the others will proceed, but I will do all that is in my power to support Richard. You know he has always been like a brother to me, and he is Georgiana's guardian. I hope you understand that I cannot allow him to be harmed any more than I could allow it to happen to my wife or my sister." He smiled sadly at his aunt. "And whether you and my uncle are happy about the fact or not, Miss Bennet is now my sister."

Lady Matlock sighed. "I have told Richard that I will give him my support where I am able, so, if I can be of assistance, please, let me know."

Darcy looked at her in surprise. "You will support him?"

"He is my son, and I cannot bear to see him in pain as I saw today." She motioned toward Richard's retreating form. "Save for when your mother and father died, my son has not cried since he was ten. At least, not that anyone has seen. However, less than half an hour ago, he sat amongst a group of women with tears in his eyes." She briefly explained all that had happened prior to Darcy's arrival at the modiste shop. "He loves her too greatly. How can I be a party to such hurt?"

Darcy stared at the door to Mrs. Havelston's shop for a moment. His aunt needed to know that her son was not the only one whose love was great. "She sold the designs for him," he said softly. "No one is supposed to know about the arrangement, so I am telling you in strictest confidence." He sighed. He knew that Miss Bingley and her friends would use the information, whether it was true or not, to disparage Kitty.

"What do you mean, she sold them for him? How would her selling designs assist Richard?"

"She spoke to me at Rycroft's wedding breakfast and asked me to invest the money she made from her sales. It was her hope that, someday, she would have enough set aside to help Richard do what he loves, and, perhaps, with any luck, she hoped he might still be free to marry her."

"But that would take years, would it not?" his aunt asked in surprise.

"She knew that." Darcy motioned to Lady Matlock's carriage. "It is time for me to go collect Richard."

She took his proffered arm. "Surely, Miss Bennet would marry, and the plan would come to naught. I cannot believe a husband would allow his wife to continue saving money for another man. No matter how noble the reason."

"She did not plan to marry if she could not marry Richard," he said as he handed his aunt into her carriage.

"But she is so young," Lady Matlock protested.

"And so very much in love," countered Darcy. "So very much in love," he repeated as he closed the door.

Chapter 13

MRS. GARDINER PLACED THE tray, which she held, on the table next to Kitty's bed and pulled a chair close. The room rested in shadows due to the curtains being drawn. A couple of candles added a bit of light so she could have read if she had felt like it, but honestly, she was too worried about Kitty to be able to concentrate on anything.

The surgeon had come, stitched up the wound, and left, yet Kitty had not woken. She sighed and placed a hand on her niece's cheek. "Kitty. Kitty, dear. I have some broth. You need to wake up."

She brushed her thumb gently along the bruise that was forming just below the corner of Kitty's left eye. The action elicited a soft groan from Kitty but no further response. Mrs. Gardiner removed her hand from her niece's cheek and, taking Kitty's hand, settled back in her chair to watch.

As she watched Kitty, she prayed until the door opened slowly, and Elizabeth and Mary slipped quietly into the room.

"How is she?" Elizabeth asked. "Mr. Darcy told us about her fall."

Her aunt sighed and rose. Kitty's fall was only part of the trouble. She motioned for Mary and Elizabeth to follow her to the opposite side of the room.

"Did he tell you about what happened before she fell?" She spoke in a hushed tone. She did not want to upset Kitty. Those three ladies at Mrs. Havelston's and that article in the paper had done enough of that. While it was true that Kitty was not awake, that did not mean she could not hear what was being said.

"He did."

Mrs. Gardiner glanced over her shoulder toward the bed. "She groans. Her eyes flutter open occasionally, but there is very little other response, save for some tears. I fear the injury to her heart is a far greater concern than the one to her head."

Both Elizabeth and Mary sucked in a quick breath.

"Do you fear that she will not wake?" Mary asked.

"I do." Mrs. Gardiner sighed. A broken heart was a dangerous thing. "If he were to come..."

Elizabeth placed an arm around her aunt's shoulders. "Hers is not the only heart that has been injured. My husband fears to leave his cousin alone. I will ask Fitzwilliam if he thinks Richard should visit. I am not opposed to it."

"Nor am I," Mrs. Gardiner agreed. "Although it will not solve the issue of his announced betrothal."

"It is incomprehensible to me that a father should treat his son so." Mary shook her head. Disgust was clearly etched in her features.

"Indeed, it is," Mrs. Gardiner agreed. "Now, come. I will send for some tea, and we shall have a lovely chat." She took each by the arm and led them back to Kitty's bed.

"Kitty, darling," she said as Elizabeth and Mary found seats on the bed, one on either side of Kitty's feet, "your sisters have come to call, and we are going to have tea. Would you care for some?"

Mrs. Gardiner waited a moment just in case there was a response before continuing. "Very good, I shall have four cups sent up, just in case you change your mind. We would dearly love to share some with you."

"Tell me about your day," Mrs. Gardiner said after she had rung for the tea.

In hushed tones, they began a conversation about the very mundane aspects of life, being very careful to keep the topic something that was either cheery or non-troubling. Tension that could be felt hung around them.

Just as the tea was being delivered by a maid, Kitty began to toss her head as if troubled by a dream.

"It cannot be true," she muttered in a sleepy, slurred voice.

"Katherine," Mary scooted up on the bed until she could smooth Kitty's hair back away from her face. The motion seemed to calm her sister. "Katherine," she continued, "it is true."

Both Mrs. Gardiner and Elizabeth gasped.

"She wants – nay, needs – to hear the truth even if it is unpleasant."

"I am not so certain," Mrs. Gardiner said.

"I know it in my heart." Tears clung to the rims of Mary's eyes.

Mrs. Gardiner gave her a small smile and a nod. Mary was not the sort of sister to hurt a sister unnecessarily. She could be firm and unmoving, but her heart was not hard.

"Colonel Fitzwilliam's father has done a horrible thing in printing that announcement." Mary reached down and lifted one of Kitty's hands to her lips to kiss it. "It is a wrong that must be righted, and my dear, it would help us ever so much if you would wake up so that we could worry together about how to fix this mess." She kissed her sister's hand once again and lifted it to her cheek. "Please. We need you." A tear slid down her cheek and onto her sister's hand.

Kitty's hand flinched slightly, and her eyes opened briefly.

"Are you awake?" Mary asked softly.

Kitty's mind began to lift from where it had been trapped. She nodded her head but just barely. Still, it was enough to make her gasp. Oh! It hurt so much!

"Oh, my dear girl," she heard her aunt's voice near her, stirring her senses even more.

"Kitty."

Was that Elizabeth calling her? Were they all there? She attempted to force her eyes open. Through her lashes, she could make out the forms of two of her sisters and her aunt hovering around her.

It was true. The thought penetrated her foggy thinking, causing her to want to slip away from the reality of it again, but the tears she felt on her hand as it rested against Mary's cheek would not allow her to retreat.

Slowly, she opened her eyes, blinking in the dim light of the candles. "It is true?" she whispered, hoping that it had merely been a bad dream.

"It is," Mary said, "but it is not finished. We must have hope that things will right themselves with a little help."

The door opened, admitting Jane to the room. "Is she well?" she asked.

"No," Kitty answered. "My head hurts. My eye on one side will not fully open, and I feel as if someone is crushing my chest."

"Oh, but you will be well," Mary said. "I shall see to it." She placed Kitty's hand back on the bed. "Can you sit?" she asked.

"I do not know." Kitty shifted and pushed up on her arms. The pain the motion caused was unpleasant, but the spinning in her head was nearly unbearable. "Oh, the room will not stay still." She closed her eyes as she settled back against the head of the bed. "Ah, that is better."

"You do not need to see to drink." Mary wrapped one of Kitty's hands around the cup she held. "I will not let the cup fall, but you must guide it so that I do not pour it all down the front of you."

She took a few sips. The broth was comfortingly warm, but her stomach was not overly pleased to accept it. "I cannot drink more."

"Then, you will not." Mary's words were gentle. "Perhaps you can lie down again?"

That sounded like a wonderful idea, and Elizabeth helped her to do as Mary suggested.

"Has my husband come with you?" Elizabeth asked Jane as she fiddled with Kitty's pillows, making certain that she was as comfortable as possible.

Jane shook her head, but her eyes sparkled. It was rare to see Jane looking so mischievous.

"No, he and my husband have gone to call on Hurst." She joined Mary and Elizabeth on the bed, sitting between them and directly at the end of Kitty's feet. "I dare say we will be rid of Caroline soon." She smiled widely.

"Charles may be all that is amiable and pleasant, but it seems when pushed beyond his limits, he can be quite the opposite." Jane giggled. "Caroline will be married within in a month, or she will be sent to Scarborough and expected to find a husband there."

She sighed. "I know I should not be so happy about it, but she has been terribly hateful to so many of my sisters." She rested a hand on Kitty's foot and gave it a gentle squeeze.

"Well, I, for one, am glad to hear it," Mary said.

Kitty blinked. Her head must be more injured than she thought. Mary had not just said she was happy that Miss Bingley was being sent away, had she?

"Do not look so shocked," Mary continued.

Apparently, Kitty had heard correctly.

"Miss Bingley is only reaping what she has sown, as is right and proper." Mary gave a sharp, decisive nod of her head to emphasize how greatly she believed what she had said.

The action made Kitty smile. "I think it is better than she deserves. She is hateful."

Jane winked at her and then looked at Mary and Elizabeth as if she had the best secret to share. "It is worse than it sounds," she whispered. She leaned forward toward Kitty and the others followed suit.

"I am sure I was not supposed to hear this part, but Charles intends to seek out Mr. Blackmoore." She grinned widely as her sisters gasped. "He ended his conversation about it with 'and I do not care if he has to compromise her to make her agree.'"

"Oh, my!" Mrs. Gardiner cried.

"Indeed," Jane replied happily. "Caroline will not be able to say a word about any other compromises if she falls into one herself."

"If only the same could happen for her friends," Kitty muttered.

Mary and Elizabeth nodded their agreement, and then, at Jane's look of confusion, the three of them took turns telling her all they knew about Miss Ivison and Miss Pearce.

Chapter 14

"ONE PROBLEM IS WELL-IN-HAND," Darcy said upon entering Rycroft's sitting room. He gave his aunt a kiss and nodded his acceptance of a drink from Rycroft. He shot Richard a questioning look.

Richard lifted one shoulder and let it drop in response to the unspoken question. He was not better nor was he any worse.

"Bingley and Hurst are calling on Blackmoore," Darcy continued, "to see if he is still in need of a wife – one with acceptable connections, a tidy fortune, and who will be happy to be a baroness one day, no matter the arrangements at home."

"Will Mr. Blackmoore keep his mistress?"

"Georgiana," Richard said in unison with Darcy and Rycroft.

"I know there are gentlemen who keep them."

"I wish you did not know that." Darcy took a large gulp of his drink.

Richard, on the other hand, was glad that Georgiana was not unaware of such things. But then, he was her cousin and not her doting older brother who struggled to see her as anything other than the sweet younger sister she was.

"And I wish it did not happen," Georgiana replied with a shrug. "I cannot imagine having to abide such an arrangement."

Darcy groaned.

Georgiana smiled at him reassuringly. "There is no need to worry, Fitzwilliam. I have learned many things over the past year about men, and I can promise you that any gentleman who keeps a mistress will not on my list of possible suitors, for I shall not abide such a man. A man who touches another woman shall not touch me."

Darcy squeezed his eyes shut as if in pain. "Could we please speak of something else?" he begged.

"If you wish," Georgiana replied.

Richard could not help the smile that crept onto his lips at the look of relief on Darcy's face to have the topic turn from his sister becoming a lady of marriageable age.

He leaned against the frame of the window and stared out into the darkness that was descending on the city. He peered as far up the street and then down as he could see from his vantage point. Bingley was to see the ladies home from their aunt's house, and Richard knew when they returned, they would have news about Kitty.

He glanced at Darcy, who was still watching him warily.

Once Bingley returned, Richard would convince the others – most especially Darcy – that he was capable of not doing himself harm, and he would be allowed to return to his rented room where he could wallow in his sorrow privately.

He closed his eyes and leaned his head against the frame of the window, attempting to find some peace, but it was no use. No matter how much he tried to think about something, anything, else, he saw Katherine, lips trembling, eyes filled with tears, telling him he had her heart and then, turning away.

"I would like to take a walk." Lady Sophia slipped her arm through his. "I find this room to be rather boisterous." She gave him a meaningful look and motioned toward the door with her head. "There are a great deal more rooms in this house that are far less crowded."

If his aunt wanted to offer a moment of escape from the watchful eyes of his cousins, he was not going to refuse. So, pushing off the window frame, he allowed her to lead him from the room.

"Reginald is correct," she said as they strolled down the hall. "I do have something that may help sway your father from his position. It is in my apartment if you care to see it."

Richard turned toward the grand staircase. "I will take whatever help and hope you can give."

"My brother, your father, has been a selfish creature all his life. You should have seen the airs he would put on when we were young. It is a miracle he lived to ascend to the title." She chuckled. "Reginald may have taken orders when he was first enlisted in the navy, but it was never his lot to be on the receiving end of commands. He was always destined to be the one giving them. So, you can imagine the scuffles that took place when your father had pushed his eldest son and heir role too far."

Richard smiled despite himself. He would have liked to have seen his father on the receiving end of some unpleasantness.

"Catherine was just as bad." She shook her head. "She lorded her position over Anne and me and gave us instruction on things about which she knew little more than we did." She sighed. "And her lectures about propriety were more than sufficient to bore even our tried-and-true governess to tears." She laughed. "Catherine was constantly telling Miss Blair how the lessons were being presented incorrectly. It is a wonder the lady stayed with us all those years. I dare say my mother paid her handsomely not to leave."

She drew her key from her pocket and opened the door to her sitting room. "I was glad that Catherine was married before I had my come out. Anne was not so fortunate. Oh, the trials she endured! Catherine was determined to select a husband for Anne, and, as you can imagine, she was not pleased that Anne chose to fall in love with a mere mister, a very wealthy and well-connected mister, but one who was sadly lacking a title."

She pulled out a drawer of her desk and laid it aside. Then, she bent to look into where the drawer had been and reached to the back. Two clicks and she had a small box in her hand. "One of my many secret treasures," she said with a smile as she handed Richard the box.

Richard took the box and, after examining the detail of it, removed the lid, revealing a golden necklace. He lifted it by its chain, suspending it in front of him until he had placed the box back on the desk. Then, he let the pendant, a heart made of woven and twisted gold, drop into his hand.

"It was my mother's," Lady Sophia explained.

"It is beautiful."

"I hope to one day give it to Mary."

"She would like it."

Lady Sophia nodded. "There is another necklace just like it somewhere in this world."

"Did the jeweler make many?" Richard lifted it again and studied the craftsmanship of the heart. The weaving of the metal reminded him somewhat of a bird cage, but instead of a bird, there was a pearl locked away in the center.

"He made only two, and at my mother's request, he destroyed his mold after the second was cast."

Richard watched the heart twirl at the end of the chain. "This is the necklace she wears in her portrait, is it not?"

"It is." Lady Sophia took the necklace from him. "It was a memento of a lost love. Rare as the pearl, precious as the gold that encircles it. That is what Mother would always say to me when I would play with it as a girl." She lay the necklace gently back in the box. "It is the kind of love she told me to seek and the kind you have found."

She motioned for him to have a seat and then sat beside him on the couch. "My mother was devastated when the necklace went missing from her room. She thought it had been stolen by her maid, and so the maid was dismissed without reference. However, it later appeared in Reginald's room. My brother pled his innocence, but my mother and father were furious with him and sent him away to sea." She shrugged sadly. "My brother, your father, told his father that Reginald had taken the necklace to give to a lover, a woman, he claimed, who was of inferior standing, a shop girl."

"Julie," Richard said softly.

"That is the name I heard." She gave him a quizzical look. "She exists?"

He nodded. "She is now a modiste. You know her as Mrs. Havelston."

Lady Sophia gasped, and her eyes grew wide. "The woman who made Mary's gowns?"

"She is also my mother's modiste," Richard said.

Lady Sophia chuckled wryly and shook her head. "Your father must not be aware of the connection. I cannot imagine him allowing your mother to support that fortune seeking adventurist, I believe that is what my father called her." She patted his hand. "However, that is not what makes this necklace a source of influence."

She stopped and thought for a moment. "Or perhaps it makes it an even greater one." She shook her head. "Reginald had not taken the necklace. It was your father who had taken it to pay a gaming debt. However, when the news of it having been stolen fell on the wrong ears so that the necklace could no longer be used as payment for his debt, and after a rather heated argument between my brothers, the necklace found its way into Reginald's room to be discovered by a maid who was more than a little friendly with your father." She raised an eyebrow and pursed her lips in displeasure.

"So, you know the truth, but Uncle Reginald does not."

"My eldest brother told me he was not above forcing me to marry someone of his choosing by arranging a compromise. And since I was already in love with my Lord Rycroft and hopeful of an offer, I kept his secret." She shrugged. "After I was married, his threat held little weight, but Reginald seemed happy at sea, so I never told him. Perhaps I should have." She shoved the box at Richard as if it were coal that burnt her hand. "I had hoped this would help you, but oh, my, Reginald will be so displeased."

"I think he would understand. It is not as if being cleared of the wrongdoing would have made it possible for him to marry Mrs. Havelston." He opened the box and looked inside once again at the beautiful heart. "You said there were two made. If grandmother had one, what became of the second?"

"She gave the second necklace to a particular groomsman who was not long after dismissed from the stables at Matlock House. That necklace was accompanied by a note explaining its importance to both her and two of her children to act as a protection of sorts for him should he need it. It was her way of keeping her husband from pursuing him any further than having him dismissed from his position."

"Do you mean to tell me that the rumours of an affair are true?"

Lady Sophia nodded.

"But could my grandfather not just take the necklace and note from the man?"

She smiled. "Your grandmother was clever. You see, it was when she suspected she was with child, shortly before she married your grandfather, that she gave the necklace to her lover with the instructions that he hide it and the note in a safe place known only to him and one other. She never told her husband what the memento was that she had given to the man, just that it had been given with a note that could damage the reputation of the child she carried, who was by then thought to be heir to the Earl of Matlock."

"Did no one question the timing of the birth?"

Lady Sophia shook her head. "Your grandmother carried twins, your father and Catherine. It is not uncommon for twins to arrive early. Until she told me the story when she passed the necklace on to me shortly before she died, I had no idea that I did not share a father with my two eldest siblings. I had heard rumours of infidelity and seen some amorous exchanges between her and other gentlemen, but I had thought my father would have thrown her out if it were true that she had borne him another man's child. However, I suspect it was easier to accept them as his own and save his reputation than to send them away, and she had made sure he could not send them away quietly, since she had happily proclaimed her good fortune of being with child to one and all. She was clever."

Richard heartily agreed with that assessment. His grandmother had seemingly thought of everything needed to ensure the security of herself and her children, as well as the safety of her lover. "You do not know what happened to this man?"

"I have no idea what became of him, and if she did, she never spoke a word of it."

"And this," Richard held up the box, "has the potential to cause a rift between brothers and, if the other necklace were found, to bring embarrassment to my father?"

"He could lose his title if Reginald cared to put forth a challenge, which he might."

"But only if the other necklace were ever found?"

"An unlikely event after all these years." Lady Sophia stood and smoothed her skirts. "However, the threat of my telling his brother of the truth of that necklace," she pointed to the box, "has on occasion swayed your father's position."

Richard turned the box over in his hand as he began contemplating how best to use the information he now possessed. It was a decision that would take some time and thought, and so standing, he handed the box back to her. "Tuck it away again until I need it."

She smiled and did as he suggested.

"Shall we go see if Lady Rycroft or Mrs. Darcy have returned with news about your lady?"

His aunt slipped her arm through his after locking her door.

"You shall marry her," she whispered, "even if I have to stuff you both in my carriage and whisk you off to Gretna Green by myself."

Chapter 15

RICHARD PICKED UP THE bottle of port and eyed the glass that sat on the table in his rented room. He had planned to consume much of the bottle last night when he had acquired it from Mr. Wood.

However, knowing Kitty had awakened and that he had some hope of swaying his father's position, coupled with the fact that an excess of drink would muddle his thinking for more than the night, he had refrained. One could not properly plan strategy while one's brain was muddled, after all, and he was not giving up Kitty before exhausting every option either he or his relations could contrive. Therefore, in the end, he has settled for just two smallish glasses of port before casting himself into bed.

Be that as it may...

He removed the cork and poured a measure of the sweet, red wine into the glass — a little bit for fortification for the day that lay ahead might be a good idea. He replaced the stopper and sat himself down to drink and attempt to think of nothing else save the richness of his beverage. What to do about his future could be considered later.

He had done a fair bit of thinking on the subject while he should have been sleeping in the wee hours of the morning, and he had come to the conclusion that he would only use the necklace if... or rather, when... it became necessary, for there would likely would be a point where there would be no other option but to put it forward and reveal the whole secret to the admiral.

Just as he was draining the last drops from the glass, having done a very poor job of not thinking about what lay ahead, there came a stomping on the stairs, followed by a loud knocking at his door.

"Fitzwilliam," Rycroft called. "Open the door! It is of great importance."

Richard opened the door and scowled at his cousin. "Your stomping and shouting are most unsettling for this time of day."

Rycroft pushed his way into the room and began gathering Richard's coat and hat. "To put it bluntly, I do not give a farthing about unsettling your day." He shoved the coat at Richard. "Put it on."

Richard's brows rose. It was unlike his cousin to be so demanding. "What has you in a temper?"

"I should be in bed with my wife, but instead, I have been sent to collect you."

Richard bit back a smile at the look of utter frustration on his cousin's face. "And why must I be collected?"

"I am not exactly sure. I honestly was not listening as I ought to have been." He waved a hand in the air. "It has something to do with the paper and your father. I have never been particularly good at listening to Aunt Catherine when she is in a dither."

"Aunt Catherine?" Richard took his hat from Rycroft.

"Yes." He leveled another less than pleased look at Richard. However, this one was not directed at Richard. The roll of Rycroft's eyes before he began speaking again was the telltale sign that this one was meant for their aunt. "She appeared at my home demanding to see you. Apparently, Darcy's butler is better prepared to handle her, as she did not gain admittance to Darcy House," he grumbled.

"I would not blame your staff too much. She was probably in no mood to be put off by the time she reached your home if she was unsuccessful at Darcy's." And their aunt in a mood was not the sort of woman capable of being refused by many.

"Most likely." Rycroft held the door open for Richard. "If you would be so kind as to hurry. Until I have produced you and our aunt has been satisfied..."

Richard held up a hand. "I know. You do not need to explain." He locked the door and descended the stairs as quickly as he could.

"I see you found him, and in one piece." Mr. Wood met them in the entry with his wife beside him.

"You mustn't begin your day without a bit of food." Mrs. Wood held out a small parcel to Richard. "A bit of cheese and a roll. It's not much, but it should help settle your stomach."

Rycroft stopped mid-step and spun to look at Richard. "Are you unwell?"

"Most of us men are after a few too many drinks," Mr. Wood replied.

"I did not have as many as I had planned."

"That is good to hear. I wish you well." Mr. Wood held the door open for Rycroft and Richard.

"Thank you for the port, and the breakfast," Richard said as he followed his cousin out of number eight Bartlett's Buildings.

Rycroft climbed into his carriage and shook his head. "I was not thinking," he said apologetically. "I am afraid I have forgotten rather quickly the fear of losing one's love. I am sorry."

Richard waved his cousin's words away. He did not wish to speak of his loss. "It is understandable when one has been granted the blessing of happiness."

Rycroft groaned. "That is another thing I should not have mentioned, I suppose."

"I do not wish for you all to treat me with pity," Richard growled.

Rycroft's eyes searched Richard's expression before he nodded and said, "You should eat. Our aunt is difficult enough to endure under good circumstances."

Richard untied the cloth and broke off a bit of the roll. He hoped it did help settle his stomach, for it would be nice to have at least one part of his body feeling settled.

Rycroft waited until he had put the food in his mouth before he spoke. "I was not speaking of pitying you. I was speaking of being considerate. I was not considerate, as I was, in fact, only thinking of myself." He leaned his head back. "However, if you would like to pity me, you may, for I find I am feeling quite sorry for myself and would enjoy the company."

Richard rolled his eyes. He knew that his cousin was not being as selfish as he sounded. As was often the case,

Rycroft was attempting to lighten the unease of another by painting himself in an unflattering light.

"If you wish to have someone with whom to share that particular type of misery, I suggest we stop at Darcy's and drag him along. I am afraid I may never be able to join you in such misery, as there is reason to believe that I will never have a wife with whom I wish to lie in bed all day." He broke off another piece of roll. "Ouch!"

"I beg your pardon."

"It was no accident," Richard snapped as he rubbed the shin Rycroft had kicked.

Rycroft shrugged. "Perhaps it was not, but it was well-deserved. You should not speak such lies." He leveled a glare at Richard. "You will marry for love. Has my mother not already said as much?"

Richard nodded. "But it is not settled that it will be." He wanted to believe that the necklace would be enough to purchase what he longed for with all his heart, but he did not trust that his father would not find some way to make it impossible.

"You know my mother. It will be done. Very little will stand in her way... including your father." Rycroft leaned his head against the back of the carriage once again. "Finish your food. Mary will be displeased if she hears I took you away without allowing you to break your fast." His head popped off the wall of the carriage. "And when I call for tea, drink some." He leaned his head back again, a small smile creeping its way onto his lips as he closed his eyes.

Richard gave his head an amused shake. It was good to see his cousin so happy even if it made his own heart ache just a bit more.

~*~

"This is your fault!" Lady Catherine jabbed her finger in Richard's face as he entered the drawing room at Rycroft Place.

"It is lovely to see you as well, Aunt," he said wryly before greeting the rest of the occupants of the room.

Lady Catherine huffed. "If you had just agreed to marry Anne, none of this would have happened!" She snatched a newspaper off a chair and flung it at him before plopping, in a rather unladylike fashion, into that chair. "She is ruined. Utterly ruined."

Richard picked up the paper and searched for whatever it was he was supposed to see. Rycroft stood at his shoulder.

"Oh!" Rycroft's tone was one of surprised amusement as he tapped an announcement. "I see our cousin has a mind of her own after all."

Lady Catherine made a thoroughly unladylike sound of displeasure.

Richard laughed as he read what Rycroft had pointed out. "I do not see how this is my fault. I am not the one responsible for the 'grievous error in announcing the betrothal of Colonel Fitzwilliam and Miss de Bourgh,' nor am I the one who placed an advertisement for a husband."

He took a seat across from his aunt. There was a seat next to her. However, after having had his ears tugged and hands swatted many times over the years, he decided the safest option would be to sit where she could not reach him, for he was certain that her disgruntled mien mingled with his equally foul mood would result in sore ears and hands, at a minimum.

He folded the paper and read the announcement once again.

It is with a heavy heart that this paper must inform the public of a grievous error which was made in announcing the betrothal of Colonel Richard Fitzwilliam and Miss Anne de Bourgh. No such agreement exists, nor is it an agreement into which either party is willing to enter. However, Miss de Bourgh, an heiress in her own right, does wish to inform those Christian gentlemen of good reputation and having in their possession a title, as well as solvent and accurate financial reports, that she is willing to accept correspondence and calls with the intent of reaching a marriage arrangement. Please be advised that references and documentation showing an adherence to the above criteria will be required.

Richard chuckled and lay the paper aside. Perhaps his future would not be as difficult to claim as he expected it to be. He allowed a sliver of hope to tentatively take root in his heart.

"Rycroft, did you not promise me a cup of tea?" He crossed one leg over the other.

"Indeed, I did." His cousin gave him a grateful smile. "I am afraid I rushed Richard along to get him here as quickly as possible."

Mary lifted a brow at her husband and then tilted her head and narrowed her eyes slightly before asking, "Have you eaten?" Her question was directed at Richard, but her eyes remained on Rycroft, and a teasing smile graced her lips.

Richard smiled. "I have, thank you."

Chapter 16

"Tea at a time like this? Does no one care that my daughter's reputation is in tatters because of him?" Lady Catherine stabbed the air in Richard's direction.

"As our nephew has said, Sister, this is not his fault. The fault lies squarely on the shoulders of whoever made the erroneous announcement, as well as any party to the original agreement that was made, quite obviously, without the consent of either Anne or Richard." Lady Sophia sighed and shook her head. "While I imagine the larger part of the blame falls to our brother, I cannot help but think the advertisement for a husband is due in large part to the young lady's mother never giving her a proper come out."

The room collectively held its breath as they watched Lady Catherine's face turn a deep shade of red. Her eyes narrowed. Her lips became a tight line.

Lady Sophia calmly tilted her head to the side and waited expectantly for her sister to respond.

"Her health would not allow it. She is of a delicate constitution which would have found the rigours of a season far too overwhelming."

Richard nearly caught his laugh of disbelief – nearly.

"It is true." Lady Catherine turned toward him.

"I apologize, Aunt, but I cannot reconcile a lady of a delicate constitution with a lady who has the temerity to announce her refusal of one marriage offer and in the same breath ask for another." He accepted a cup of tea from Mary and took a sip. "I find I am quite pleased by her boldness."

Lady Catherine huffed. "You needn't be so pleased. Your father was creating a list of gentlemen with unwed daughters on whom he wished to call when I left."

Richard took a few more sips of his tea and contemplated that piece of news. He had known it would be unlike his father to quit a matter so easily. He looked at Lady Sophia and smiled. "I believe, Aunt, that it is time my father and I had a *particular* discussion."

He cast a sidelong look at his uncle Reginald and waited for Lady Sophia to give him approval. He would not do this without her consent, for he knew that it held the potential to cause a good bit of family strife.

"A splendid idea, Richard," Lady Sophia said. "And I wish to come with you. Samuel, we will use your carriage. Reginald, would you ride with us?"

Richard's eyes must have shown his surprise, for she smiled and added softly when she had risen and was standing beside him, "Your father will be more compliant if we have Reginald in the sitting room."

Richard smiled and shook his head. "You are well-versed in strategy."

She leaned closer. There was a twinkle in her eye. "How do you suppose so many of my young friends have found themselves happily married?" She pulled on her gloves. "Some people play chess. I do not. I have the season."

"What about Anne?" Lady Catherine crossed the room toward them. "What am I to do about Anne?"

Lady Sophia turned toward her sister. "I would make sure tea is served at the interviews and that she is shown to best advantage."

"Interviews?" Lady Catherine said in surprise.

"There will be callers. Anne is an heiress, the daughter of a baronet, and the niece of the Earl of Matlock. One of those things would make her an attractive choice to many gentlemen, but when you combine them, she will have a surfeit of suitors." Taking in her sister's calculating gleam, she added, "I would not, however, try to make the choice for her, since she obviously has a mind of her own and is not afraid to exert her opinions."

"But..." Lady Catherine grabbed Lady Sophia's arm. "But I do not know how to show her to best advantage." Though her voice was soft, barely above a whisper, there was no missing the panic that filled her.

Lady Sophia patted the hand that lay on her arm. "Catherine, that is of your own doing; however, I am not without some compassion for my niece." Her hand stilled but remained on top of Lady Catherine's.

Richard noted the way her brow rose slightly, and her mouth curved into a small smile, and he knew she was preparing some bit of strategy as she stood quietly for a moment.

Finally, she gave her sister's hand another pat and said, "I will help Anne, if, and only if, you help Richard and Miss Bennet."

Lady Catherine's eyes grew wide. "Miss Bennet?"

"Yes, Miss Bennet, the young lady whom Richard would like to marry."

Lady Catherine darted a look at Richard before giving a small shake of her head. "I tried to warn him about Mrs. Bennet. I told him to accept Mrs. Darcy and Lady Rycroft without hesitation, but he would not listen." She tapped her hand over her heart. "Oh my, I feel quite ill."

And she did look it. The colour had drained completely from her face, and her breathing had become noticeable, as if taking in air were a challenge. Richard took her by the arm and led her to a chaise. "A bit of wine," he said to Rycroft.

"Salts," Mary ordered, "then the wine." She took the newspaper from where Richard had discarded it and began to fan Lady Catherine. "My mother suffers from fits of nerves," she explained. "A few moments of quiet, combined with a fan, some salts, and a glass of wine have always been effective."

Richard watched as Mary took charge and soon had his aunt looking decidedly less ill.

"It would be best if she were to return to Matlock House and retire for a rest." Mary directed the comment to Richard and then turned back to Lady Catherine. "However, I am curious to know something, if I may, your ladyship." She waited to receive permission before continuing. "You mentioned that you advised Lord Matlock to accept both my sister and me. Is it because of what my mother said when you visited Longbourn?"

Lady Catherine closed her eyes and began to look faint once again as she nodded.

"Then," Mary's voice was soft, "I would suggest you try again to convince Lord Matlock to accept my family, not for my sake, nor even for the sake of my sister Elizabeth, but for the sakes of Colonel Fitzwilliam and my sister Kitty." She bit her lip as if unsure if she should continue, but after a short pause, she did. "I have seen the necklace. The delicate weaving of the gold is exquisite and not easily forgotten."

Richard felt Lady Sophia's hand grasp his shoulder from where she stood behind him.

Lady Catherine drew a deep breath and moved to stand. "You are quite right, Lady Rycroft. It would be best if that necklace were not seen again."

"Do not move," Admiral Fitzwilliam commanded before she could rise. "Do you mean to tell me that the rumours of my mother having a paramour are true?"

Lady Catherine bowed her head and looked at her hands which were clasped firmly in her lap. "Yes." She peeked up at him. "I did not know of their truth until I attempted to stop Darcy's marriage."

The admiral opened his mouth to speak and then closed it again. He raised his finger as if he were going to make a point and then lowered it. Finally, he gave a curt nod of his head as if he had decided upon something and extended his hand to Lady Catherine.

"We have a meeting with Lord Matlock. One that it seems is long overdue." A smile spread across his face. "Oh, how I shall enjoy this. How often has he lorded his rank over me?" He chuckled. "And to think that all this time, it should have been I who was above him." He tucked her hand into the crook of his arm and patted it. "Do not fear, Sister, as long as he is reasonable, this matter shall stay a family affair."

Lady Catherine huffed. "When has our brother ever been reasonable, Reginald?"

He raised an eyebrow at her comment.

"Oh, he may have favoured me because we were twins, but he did not let me forget that I was not only second born but also female. No matter how loudly I object to anything, he nearly always ignores me."

"Unless," the admiral said, "it is in his best interest to agree."

"Precisely," Lady Catherine agreed with a further huff before beginning a diatribe about her brother, that announcement, and her daughter's future as she exited the sitting room.

"She is well recovered," Richard muttered to Lady Sophia as they followed Lady Catherine from the room.

Lady Sophia sighed and patted his arm. "I fear your father will take a bit more persuasion."

~*~

Rycroft accompanied them to the door of the sitting room, but being unwilling to leave Mary alone and not wishing to prolong his guest's departure, he called out his good wishes for their success and watched as his relations left from there. Then, as the door was closed behind the last person, he turned back to Mary.

"Are you well?" he asked as he knelt beside the chair where she sat, looking rather confused.

She shook her head. "I do not understand exactly what has happened. I knew that the necklace and the accompanying note cast doubt on Lady Catherine's

legitimacy. That is why I referred to the necklace at all."
Her eyes were wide and filled with concern. "I had hoped
she would lend her support to my sister. I did not wish to
create any larger scandal, I can assure you."

Chuckling, Rycroft rose and pulled her up into his
embrace. "My dear Lady Rycroft, it seems you are as
proficient at starting scandals as I." He stopped her protest
with a kiss. Sighing contentedly as he broke the kiss, he
held her for a moment.

"Lady Catherine and Lord Matlock are twins," he said
at last, "so your revelation concerning the necklace that
my grandmother gave to her lover casts doubt not only on
the legitimacy of my aunt but also my uncle. And, if the
admiral were to be of the vicious sort — and I assure you he
is not — he could challenge his brother's right to inherit."

"Oh." Mary's voice was filled with remorse. "If he does
challenge it, what shall become of Lady Matlock and her
children?" She pursed her lips and shook her head. "I
should not have said anything."

Rycroft tilted her chin so that she was looking at him.
"You did nothing wrong," he said firmly. "It is a secret
that has been kept too long. Strong words will be hurled,
threats will be made, but Lord Matlock will capitulate to
whatever demands the admiral makes. And then, all will be
well, or at least, as well as can be expected in this family."

"You are certain?"

"As certain as one can be." He kissed her forehead and
then the tip of her nose. A rakish smile spread across his
face. "I, however, am the rightful heir to my title and as
such, have a duty to it." He bent and scooped her into
his arms. "It is a duty that I dare not shirk." And despite

her protests that it was most improper to be carrying her through the house and up the stairs, he did just that.

Chapter 17

LORD MATLOCK LOOKED UP briefly from his desk as Richard entered his study. He gave a slight nod and scowl as he waved to a chair. "I had not thought I would see you for a few more days."

"Did you not?" Richard took a seat.

His uncle Reginald had wished to confront his brother immediately upon entering Matlock House, but after a few words with Lady Sophia in the carriage, he had agreed to let Richard speak to Lord Matlock first.

"I am surprised you did not expect me yesterday what with that announcement in the paper and all." Richard lifted his chin and peered down his nose slightly at his father the way he might if he were dealing with one of his recruits. He had determined before entering the study that he would not act the part of a son, but rather of a man of rank and position, which he was. It was high time his father remembered that.

"Yes, well, that has come to naught now, has it not?" His father placed his pen in its holder. "Foolish girl," he muttered before leaning back in his chair and clasping his hands in front of his stomach. "I imagine you have come expecting to be free from your duty to your family since my first choice has not proven to be a good one." His lips curled in a scowl. "I have begun negotiations for another acceptable choice." He tapped the stack of correspondence to his left.

"So Lady Catherine said." However, there would be no others. His Katherine was his choice.

Richard commanded a nonchalant smile to curve his lips as he leaned forward and snatched the pile of letters from off his father's desk. Standing, he made a show of reading the name on the first letter. He did not actually look at the name. It did not matter who the lady fortunate enough to be considered good enough for Lord Matlock's second son was.

"Oh, she will not do at all." He tossed the first envelope into the fire that warmed the room. The page caught and glowed brightly before turning into sparks that rose towards the chimney.

"What are you doing?" his father cried, leaping out of his chair and rushing toward Richard.

"As a matter of fact, none of these will do." Richard tossed the full pile into the flames. He watched as the fire claimed the pages that he had fed it. "I have made my choice, and she is not any of these ladies."

His father's face was red with anger. His mouth hung open, but no sound came out.

Richard walked past him and took a seat once again. "That is why I have come. My decision is made. I am selecting my own bride. Your assistance is not required."

His father whirled toward him. "You will not see a farthing of your inheritance." He stomped over to the bell pull and gave it a firm tug.

His father's response was as expected. Richard calmly crossed one leg over the other and, once again, forced an unconcerned smile to his lips. It was an action which seemed to make Lord Matlock sputter even more about duty and foolish notions and failure. It was a tirade that only ended when the butler opened the door.

"My solicitor. I have need of him at once," Lord Matlock demanded of his butler as he glared at Richard. "Within the hour. I must see him within the hour."

"Yes," Richard agreed, "within the hour would be excellent." Again, he smiled at his father. "If you are through with your ranting, my lord, there is a matter we should discuss before Mr. Fletcher arrives."

Lord Matlock's eyes narrowed. "Very well. What have you to say for yourself?"

"Please have a seat, Father." Richard fidgeted indifferently with his cuff while he waited for him to be seated. "I had an enlightening discussion with Lady Sophia yesterday when I was feeling ..." he paused, "rather melancholy."

Lord Matlock's brows rose. "What did my sister have to say?"

"Do you not wish to know why I was melancholy?"

His father huffed and waved his hand, indicating that Richard should continue with his tale.

"Very well. I shall tell you. It seems that my father did not keep his word. He had promised me a fortnight to come to a decision, but he did not hold true to his part of the bargain." He held up a hand to keep his father from interrupting. "It was shocking to see one's life signed away in an announcement in the paper in such an underhanded and ignoble fashion. However, that was only a portion of my grief."

For the first time since walking into the room, Richard let his emotions rise to the surface and take up residence in his expression. As he leaned forward and rested his elbows on the arm of his chair, he knew his face must be conveying his displeasure well when he saw his father flinch.

"You see, the real trouble lies in the fact that I had already come to a decision and had only two nights prior declared myself to a young lady." He saw his father's eyes grow wide. "I did not wish for your money and property more than I wished for her love," he explained, although he did not know why he attempted to as he heard his father snort in derision.

"Though she knew my lot in life was not going to be one of wealth, she accepted me, so you can imagine how the news of my supposed betrothal to Anne took her by surprise. In fact, her surprise was so great that it caused her to swoon and receive an injury to her head." He drew a deep breath and released it slowly, attempting to contain the anger he felt for his father's role in Kitty's injury. "I understand that she did eventually wake yesterday; however, at the time when I was speaking to my aunt, she had not yet regained her senses."

Lord Matlock affected an air of indifference. "So, a young lady of low birth swooned and hit her head. What is that to me?"

Richard clenched his teeth as his anger struggled to be released with his desire to remain in control of himself. "She is a gentleman's daughter," he snarled at his father.

"Of wealth or title?"

"No," Richard growled, "but she is of good character."

Oh, how easy it would be to turn his back on his father at this moment and to leave in a fit of fury and to stomp and shout as he did so. But to what avail? It was not as if his father would take much notice of it. To his father, all that mattered was position and power, and so, Richard swallowed his fury so he could retain what little power he had.

"Character is of little importance when it comes to position in society, my boy."

Richard gave his father a sweeping look of assessment. "Yes, that is obvious." He did not veil his disgust; however, the tone seemed lost on his father, who merely shifted to a more relaxed position in his chair.

"Now that I have endured your little tale of woe, would you be inclined to tell me what my sister told you?"

Richard smiled, and this was not a forced smile but one of genuine pleasure. Now was the time to see his father begin to feel uneasy. Now was the time to shift the tide in this engagement, and for the mighty Lord Matlock to feel the loss of the precious power he craved.

"No, I would not be so inclined, for I find I would rather tell Admiral Fitzwilliam the tale I heard." He was pleased to see the puzzled and somewhat concerned expression on his father's face. "Lady Sophia showed me grandmother's necklace." His smile grew as his father's eyes widened in understanding. "I see you know the story of your perfidy at my uncle's expense. However, I am led to believe that the admiral does not know it." Though he likely did now since Lady Sophia was going to tell him about the necklace she had secreted away in her apartment. Be that as it may, his father did not need to know that bit of news. "That is a fact that could be easily remedied."

Lord Matlock sank back in his chair, looking decidedly ill-at-ease.

"Did you know that there were two such necklaces?" Richard rose, went to the door, and opened it. "Harrison, please, send my uncle to me," he called to the butler before closing the door once again.

"What are you doing?" Lord Matlock's voice was satisfyingly filled with panic.

"Did you know that there were two necklaces?" Richard repeated as he stood near the door waiting for his uncle's arrival.

"I had heard there might have been."

"There is no might have been about it," Richard replied. "In fact, I know where the second necklace can be found and of, at least, two people who have seen it."

Ah, there. There was terror in his father's eyes, and it was a delicious sight.

"Remember what I know about grandmother's copy of the necklace when you speak with my uncle," Richard cautioned. "I would hate to see our family ruined." He lowered his voice and took three steps toward his father. "I would not hesitate to speak of what I know, if the ruin would only affect you, but I must think of my mother and brother."

The door opened to let the admiral enter, and Richard turned to leave but stopped before his uncle and nodded toward his father. "I have had my say. He is all yours, Admiral. Do as you see fit. I will await you with my mother and aunt."

And with that, he quit the room and walked the length of the hall slowly. He needed a moment to collect his thoughts and calm his mind. There was no need to bring his anger and frustration with him to a room where emotions would likely be strained by the uncertainty of what would come from the meeting between brothers which was just now rumbling to life in Matlock House's study.

Upon reaching the door to the drawing room, he straightened his coat.

"Tea has just arrived, sir," Harrison said.

Richard nodded toward the room. "How are things?"

"It is not for me to notice, sir."

Richard cocked an eyebrow and his head at Harrison's answer. "I am not my father."

"No, sir, you are not."

Richard waited.

"There were raised voices for a bit, but things seemed to have been sorted."

Richard smiled. "I appreciate the information, Harrison. Do not fear; I shall not alert anyone to the fact that you have ears which are in working order."

"Thank you, sir." There was the hint of a smile on the man's face.

Richard clapped him on the shoulder. "Into the fray then," he said as Harrison opened the drawing room's door for him.

Chapter 18

As soon as she saw Richard at the door, his mother rose to pour him a cup of tea. It was as if she had been watching for him rather than paying attention to anything else in the room. "Was your father reasonable?" she asked as she handed him the cup.

He kissed her cheek before accepting the cup. "He never is, but I think he is ready to see reason." He took a sip of tea. "Did you tell the admiral what you knew about grandmother's necklace?" he asked Lady Sophia as he took a seat next to her on the settee next to his mother's favourite chair.

She nodded. "He was understandably angry." She looked at her hands which were folded in her lap. "If I had known..." Her voice trailed off.

Richard placed a hand on hers. "What you knew was not willingly concealed, and you thought him happy."

Her smile was sad. "I know, and he understands that."

"I believe his anger is more toward my husband," Lady Matlock said.

"As it should be," Richard muttered. There was little he felt in regard to his father save for anger and disappointment, but his mother was a different story. For her, he felt love and concern. For her, he had endured his father for years, attempting to please not him but her.

"Are you well, Mother?" He took another sip of his tea before placing it on the table next to him and leaning toward her. "You look a bit worn."

She placed her hand on his cheek as she often did when trying to comfort both herself and him. "It has been a trying two days."

"Indeed," he agreed. He chuckled as Anne came into the room and flopped into a chair with a huff. "I dare say it shall not be any less trying for some time," he whispered to his mother.

"Do sit up." Lady Catherine gave Anne a glare as she crossed the room. "If you insist on finding a husband, you must do it properly, and a proper lady does not fling herself about." Her hands waved wildly in the air as she said it.

Anne pulled herself up in her chair and folded her arms. "I shall have to add that to my list of questions. 'Are you capable of accepting a wife who does not always sit properly when at home?'"

"You shall not ask that."

"Oh, I think I shall."

"I do not know what has become of you. It must be the foul air of the city." Lady Catherine turned toward Lady Matlock. "She is so compliant when at home."

Richard bit his cheek to keep from laughing as Anne rolled her eyes when her mother was not looking.

"I avoid you when at home, Mother, as I had been doing whilst here. However, I will not sit by and allow you to marry me off to some second son." She waved her hand in Richard's direction. "My father was a baronet, and I am his only daughter. I would expect nothing less than..." She pursed her lips and tapped her fingers on the arm of the chair. "Oh, I suppose I could accept someone as low as a knight."

Her mother huffed. "A man with wealth and land is not to be overlooked."

"And which did my cousin here possess?" She crossed her arms and slouched further into her chair.

"He would have had both if he had but listened to his father." Lady Catherine's eyes narrowed. "Sit up."

Richard watched the exchange with interest. He had never heard so many words from his cousin at one time. At Rosings, she always appeared to be weak and in need of solitude. Now, he found himself smiling at her antics as she raised a brow at her mother's command and slowly pulled herself up to a semi-proper position. Then, she tilted her head and smiled as if daring her mother to speak.

"Headstrong, obstinate girl! You will be lucky to capture a fortune hunter with such an attitude. Gentlemen, especially those with a title, desire biddable wives."

Anne pulled herself up to her full height in her chair and turned first to her aunt and then, Richard. "Did Rycroft wish a biddable wife? Do you?" She looked at both expectantly.

Lady Sophia shook her head. "Samuel would not know what to do with an amenable wife. He needs a woman who can challenge him at times." She glanced at her sister. "However, though his wife shares her opinions with him, I have not seen her do so improperly. There is a difference between having your own mind and being a harridan. In fact, Lady Rycroft would be an excellent instructor. She has helped Georgiana greatly."

"Has she?" That was news to Richard.

"Indeed, she has. You would not think such a change could occur in such a short amount of time, but I think you will find your charge a more thoughtful girl for having spent time with Mary." She gave Richard a meaningful look. "There is even that mantle of uncertainty that she wore which has lifted."

"Splendid." Richard nodded as he contemplated the information. He had worried that it would take much longer before Georgiana found her sure footing again after her ordeal.

"She is one of those Bennet girls, is she not?" Lady Matlock asked softly.

Richard nodded. "Mrs. Bingley is the first; Mrs. Darcy is the second; and Lady Rycroft is the third."

She bit her lip in an uncharacteristic show of uncertainty. "I do not know if I should say it, but I was impressed with Miss Bennet the day she returned my parcel. She seemed a proper lady."

Richard smiled. He understood her cautiousness in voicing such an opinion. He was certain it was not one of which his father would approve, and unlike his cousin Anne, his mother was a tractable wife. It was what she had been taught to be. Her husband's opinions came first, and hers fell in line with his. It had always been thus. There had been moments of pause when she had wished to speak for her son. He could see it in her mannerisms, but she had maintained her composure and held her tongue as she thought was fitting a lady of her station.

"I think you would be pleased to meet the Bennets. They are all well versed in the social graces," Lady Sophia told her. "All, that is, save, perhaps, for the youngest." She cast a sidelong glance at Anne and smiled a Lady Matlock. "The youngest seems to be less compliant with society's rules." She turned toward her niece. "She is, however, very young. I dare say she is the same age as Georgiana."

Her comments were not lost on her niece, for Anne's posture straightened. "I would like to meet Lady Rycroft."

"Perhaps next week," Lady Sophia assured her. "She is just newly married, and my son is loath to share her with anyone."

Richard laughed. "No truer words have been spoken. He was none too happy to be fetching me this morning."

Lady Sophia's eyes twinkled with amusement. "He was a bit of a thunder cloud."

A dark, heavy, grumbling thunder cloud, and Richard was about to say as much when his father threw open the door to the drawing room.

"Ah, good. You are still here." He glanced around the room, but his eyes came back to rest on Richard as he pulled in a noticeable breath and straightened his waistcoat before continuing. "My solicitor will have instructions for you about how your inheritance will be handled and suggestions for how to draw up the necessary papers to present to the father of this lady to whom you are betrothed."

Richard blinked. Had he heard that correctly?

"Oh, do not look at me so. I am not fit for Bedlam. I have merely decided it would be best if you married this young lady since you have already proposed the idea to her. A broken betrothal is not something we wish to have in the papers, and the financial consequences are not something I wish to take on. While I am still not complacent with her rank, it shall have to be."

Richard's eyes shifted to the admiral, who wore a satisfied smile.

"It is true. My brother has finally found his sense." Uncle Reginald arched an eyebrow at his brother. "However, his manners have not improved perfectly, it seems."

"Is it not enough that I do what is right? Must I also be happy about it?" Lord Matlock grumbled.

"As long as your dissatisfaction does not cause *any* of my nieces or nephews to be unhappy, I do not care how miserable you are."

Lord Matlock huffed and turned to Anne. "That means you shall also be allowed to choose your husband." He swallowed, and his lips curled as if he had tasted something sour. "He must meet with the approval of your uncle, Admiral Fitzwilliam, and your aunt, Lady Sophia. He does not need to meet the approval of myself or your mother since we were both complicit in the arranging and announcing of your betrothal to Richard."

"And my nephew's commission?" the admiral prompted.

Richard's father closed his eyes tightly and rubbed the furrow between his brows. "If you wish and a suitable replacement can be found to fill your place, I will be willing to see to his generous compensation." He blew out a breath. "Your inheritance –"

"All of it," the admiral inserted, "is yours."

It was true? He as a free man to marry how he wished and without losing anything?

"I can... I can marry Katherine?" Richard stammered. "Without losing my inheritance?"

"Aye," said his uncle said with a smile. "And you may still sell your boxes if you wish. Your father will not stop you."

Richard rose to his feet. "I can truly marry her?"

"Yes." His uncle said with a laugh. "By special license, am I right, *Lord* Matlock?"

Richard did not notice the emphasis placed on his father's title or the small flinch of his father's face. He was far too overcome with his good fortune to be aware of much. He kissed first his mother, then his aunts and cousin before startling his father with a kiss on the cheek.

"Go," his uncle said as he embraced him. "Tell your lady the happy news. It will take days for the papers to be ready. I will make certain you are dealt with fairly."

"Harrison," Richard called, "My hat and coat. Immediately." He paused and turned to his uncle. "Thank you."

"Go," his uncle replied. "Take the carriage. My brother will see to my needs."

Richard took his hat and coat from Harrison. "I can marry her," he told the butler as he rushed out the door with his hat somewhat askew and his coat unbuttoned.

"I can marry her," he called to the coachman as he rushed toward him. "Gracechurch Street as quickly as possible, my good man." He settled into his seat, and with a smile firmly in place on his face, he leaned his head back, closed his eyes, and with a sigh repeated to himself his good fortune. "I can marry her."

Chapter 19

KITTY CLUTCHED THE PACKET of sketches, which she had collected from Mrs. Havelston, tightly to her chest as the large door opened in front of her.

"Miss Katherine Bennet to see his lordship." She tried to keep her voice from showing the fear she felt at coming to a place such as this.

The butler gave her an appraising look. "Is my lord expecting you?"

"No. However, I can assure you that I have rather urgent business that requires his attention." She squared her shoulders and lifted her chin as she had seen Lydia do when asking for things that others might find impossible to even consider receiving.

"Do you have a card?"

Kitty fought the urge to drop her gaze. "I do not. Please, just tell him who is here to call on him." She tried to smile as sweetly at the older gentleman as she could. "And if you do not mind, may I wait inside instead of on the step? The wind is biting, and I promise to move no further than just inside the door while I wait."

He motioned for her to enter, and then, after closing the door and telling her to wait right where she stood, he moved slowly down the hall, pausing once to turn and peer at her again.

It was odd how he had seemed to recognize her name. His scrutiny had been rather unsettling. She should be used to it by now. Everyone, especially her mother, was always weighing her features and accomplishments against those of her sisters, but no matter how often such evaluation happened, she always felt wanting.

That was why she had attempted to emulate her sisters by picking dresses like Jane and flirting like Lydia. She was sure she would not be accepted as plain old Kitty who liked to draw and would rather sit and watch a dance than partake. She smiled to herself. There was probably not one person in all of England who knew she did not relish dancing.

She sighed. Colonel Fitzwilliam would. But then, she had, on Mary's advice, been more herself with him than with any other person.

She fidgeted with her papers. She had spent several hours last night considering her life and her dreams, and she was determined that from this day forward, she would be Katherine Bennet — not Lydia's or Mary's or Elizabeth's or Jane's sister. No, today she would begin being herself with everyone.

She straightened her posture as she saw the butler approaching.

"My lord will see you. If you will follow me."

He turned and Kitty followed, stopping before entering the room to which she had been led to hand her coat and hat to Henriella.

"Miss Bennet." Lord Matlock stood behind his desk and motioned to a chair. "I am expecting my solicitor soon, but if your business is of a quick nature, we can discuss it. I do not, however, see how we can have any business to discuss, what with you being a woman and all."

"I thank you for your time, my lord. I will get as directly to the point as I am able." Kitty smoothed her skirt. She had taken care to wear her best dress today. "I assume that, as any good husband would, you see to the bills acquired by your wife's purchases?" She paused for a moment while he confirmed that he did.

"I will also assume since I have heard that you are often seen with her in public that her appearance as she stands beside you is of great importance. I mean, one cannot be looked upon as a great man with a wife who is wearing last season's styles, now can he?" Again, she waited for his acknowledgement of the fact. She knew from spending so much time with her youngest sister and her aunt Philips that appearance and appealing to one's sense of position and popularity could be used judiciously to achieve the desired end.

She tapped the packet of papers on her lap. "I have with me some designs for dresses that I happen to know your wife adores." She sighed as if the next thing was not something she wished to admit. "I have been considering keeping the sketches for myself instead of selling them to the modiste whose shop your wife frequents. In fact, I stopped by that very shop to collect these just this morning." She closed her eyes for a moment and rubbed near her eye to attempt to dull the throbbing in her head. "Forgive me, I have a slight headache."

Since she had entered the room, Lord Matlock's eyes had been drawn many times to the gash on her forehead, and they were there once again.

"I know it must look a fright," she explained, gingerly touching the scar, "but it is in such a place that I was unable to cover it with my hair." She chuckled softly as if the injury to her head was nothing with which to be overly concerned. "It will only look worse as it heals, I suppose. Bruises are never pretty." She smiled and opened her pack of papers. "But we are not here to discuss my beauty or lack thereof. We are here to talk about my designs."

Lord Matlock blinked and turned his attention away from the wound on her head for a moment. "Why would I be interested in designs?"

"Because, my lord, you have the power to decide if your wife will get to wear my designs or if they will be tucked away or, perhaps, provided to another lady." She flipped through her designs. "She was particularly enamoured with this one." She placed it on his desk. "She would look lovely in it; do you not agree?"

He picked up the sketch and examined it. "How is it that I have this power?"

Kitty's stomach fluttered, and she was unsure if she had the courage to continue. The old Kitty would not, but she was not that girl any longer.

Lord Matlock placed the paper back on the desk. His eyes once again found that gash as he waited for her answer.

Kitty swallowed and lifted her chin determinedly. "You, my lord, have something I want."

His brows rose high. "Do I?"

"You do."

"How did you do it?" He pointed to her forehead. "It is quite ugly," he muttered.

"Some news took me by surprise, my lord."

He tapped his fingers on the desk as his head nodded slowly. "Ah, so you are *that* Miss Bennet."

"I beg your pardon?"

He sighed as if being bothered by an annoying child. "I know who you are and what you want."

She could feel the heat creeping up her neck and onto her cheeks at his dismissive tone. The room was spinning a bit faster than it had been when she walked in.

"You will need to explain." She tried not to let her head lean on her hand, but it was becoming far too difficult to keep it upright between the spinning and the throbbing. Therefore, she allowed herself the luxury of not sitting entirely properly.

"You are to be my daughter. I must say I am impressed by my son's selection. You are lovely and daring, coming here to blackmail me with your sketches. Did you expect to win me over so that I would allow you to marry my son?"

Kitty groaned softly and rubbed her head. "I did not come to win the colonel's hand. I came to win his freedom."

"Freedom? I do not see how he has ever been anything but free."

She straightened herself and folded her hands primly in her lap, attempting to ignore the movement of the objects around her. His lordship was as ignorant as he was arrogant.

"My lord," she began in the most imposing tone she could muster, "if you will forgive me for being so direct, I must disagree. Neither man nor woman can be free when they are controlled by another. If you would but release him from his betrothal to his cousin and allow him to choose his own path..." She swallowed and allowed her gaze to drop. "I will give you my drawings and turn him away, if I must." She blinked at the tears that gathered.

"I am afraid I cannot."

Kitty sucked in a breath. She had failed.

Lord Matlock rose. "My solicitor will be here at any moment, and I am under the impression from others, who are as eager as you to see my son choose his own path, that you and he are to wed, and I am to allow it."

She would have shaken her head to clear the fuzziness that was settling in if she did not know it would hurt so very much. "Is he not to wed Miss de Bourgh?"

"She has withdrawn her consent. Have you not read the papers?" He held up a hand. "Of course, you have not. You are a lady." He scrunched his face slightly as if considering something. "Although my wife does follow the society pages. I am surprised you do not."

Kitty stood slowly. "My uncle rises first and takes the paper with him to his warehouse. I do not see it until the evening, my lord."

"Warehouse?" There was a tinge of horror to his surprised repetition of the word.

"Yes, my lord, my uncle is in trade."

"Indeed?" Lord Matlock did not look pleased to hear such a thing.

"I believe he is what you would call a *cit*, my lord."

Lord Matlock huffed as he came out from behind his desk, moved toward the door where he stood with his hand on the handle, and looked at her with some interest. "You seem well-spoken for the niece of a tradesman."

"My father is a gentleman, sir. Nothing less is acceptable." At least, it was not acceptable to him.

His brows rose and his lips puckered as if he had never considered such a thing before. "Very true," he agreed. "You are fascinating, Miss Bennet. I may find myself actually liking you in time."

She curtsied. "Thank you, my lord. You do me a great honour." Flattery was a fine tool to use when dealing with those who thought so well of themselves.

He straightened just a bit, puffing up a bit like the old rooster at Longbourn did when he was getting ready to crow. "Indeed, I do. You know, I pride myself on honouring those who are of slightly lower standing than myself. I suppose I could extend that to your class as well."

"We would be most appreciative, my lord. Again, I thank you." She clutched her packet of papers to her chest and began to exit through the door he held open.

"One moment, Miss Bennet. About the sketches."

"They shall be returned to Mrs. Havelston when your son is completely free to choose his own path. As I see it, my lord, you refused my offer and countered with one of your own. However, your counteroffer did not include mention of my drawings." She put a hand on the wall to steady herself.

"Now, wait just a moment," he sputtered.

"Do not fret, my lord. You may have overlooked the mention of my designs, but I fully intend to honour my promise to you as soon as Colonel Fitzwilliam is free. It is what anyone of good breeding would do, is it not?"

Lord Matlock looked confused for a moment but then agreed and bid her good day.

"Miss, you are unwell," Henriella said wrapping an arm around Kitty. "Please let Thomas and me take you home."

"No, I have one more stop to make, and then you may take me home and someone can explain to me about what Lord Matlock was speaking." She leaned on her maid as she walked. "Perhaps a short rest in the carriage before the next meeting would be advisable. Do you think we could take a short drive?"

"I will ask Thomas," Henriella said. "La, you are so pale, miss."

"Is there anything I could get for you?" Lord Matlock's butler stood in front of the door. "A small glass of wine perhaps?"

"I thank you, but I do not wish to impose."

"It is no imposition, miss." He snapped his fingers and a footman hurried over. "A bit of wine for the lady." He looked at Kitty. "He will bring it to your carriage. Your maid is correct; you do look pale. It would be best if you found rest soon."

"I thank you, Mr. —"

"Harrison, miss."

"Mr. Harrison, you have been very helpful."

"It has been a pleasure, Miss Bennet." He held the door as the two exited, and when Kitty looked back from the carriage, he was still standing there watching until she was safely inside the vehicle.

Chapter 20

"Miss." Henriella nudged Kitty sometime later, after the Gardiners' carriage had navigated the streets of London from Matlock House to the handsome townhouse in front of which it now stood. "Miss, we are here."

Kitty opened her eyes and stretched. She straightened her hat and smoothed her clothes. "Oh, I feel so much better." It was amazing what a few minutes of rest could do for sore and dizzy head. She rubbed her temples slightly. "It is only a dull ache now. It is not pounding as it was. And the world is standing still as it should be."

"I still think you should go home, miss," said Henriella.

Kitty patted her maid's hands. "I must do this before I lose my nerve or my head heals, and I regain my sense." She laughed lightly in an attempt to ease her nerves. This visit was not going to be any easier to make than the last one had been. Perhaps fortune would favour her and she would be as successful with Miss Bingley as she had been with Lord Matlock.

"Shall I attend you?"

"Yes, please. You may wait either in the room or just outside, but in case my head starts to swoon, I would prefer to have you near."

Henriella nodded and followed her mistress out of the carriage and up the steps to the Hursts' townhouse.

Kitty lifted the knocker and let it fall. Then, she turned slightly to see Henriella, who stood behind her. "I can do this, can I not?"

"You can, miss," Henriella assured her. "And when you have finished, you may go home to a cup of tea and a good sleep."

"Thank you." The promise of rest when this ordeal was done was as good as candy being dangled in front of hungry child. Bless Henriella for knowing the exact right thing to say!

Kitty managed to turn around just before the door opened to allow her entrance. "Miss Bennet to see Miss Bingley," she informed the butler. "A private audience, if possible."

"I shall see if she is home to you."

"Tell her," Kitty added as the butler turned to leave, "that I have something of value to give her."

"Yes, miss."

Kitty shifted from foot to foot. Facing Lord Matlock had been daunting, but seeing Miss Bingley was proving to be even more unnerving. She put it to the fact that she knew naught of Lord Matlock aside from his rigid conformity to social expectations. However, Miss Bingley and her cutting remarks were well-known, and knowing what surely would be hurled at her caused Kitty's stomach to flutter and her hands to twist as she waited.

"She will see you. If you will follow me."

Kitty stood behind the butler while he announced her and then stepped into the room. As she had requested, there was no other person in the room save for Miss Bingley. Kitty dipped a curtsey. "Miss Bingley, thank you for seeing me."

"I have no choice. Should my brother hear that you were here, and I turned you away, I shudder to think of what further strictures he would place upon me." She grimaced at the sight of the gash on Kitty's forehead. "I am sorry you were injured."

Although it sounded rather hollow, Kitty chose to take it as sincere. Today was not the day to dwell in the past. Today was her day to start a new beginning.

"Thank you. I know it looks dreadful." She took a seat and pulled a folded paper from her reticule. "I brought you something." She held the paper out to Miss Bingley. "I have spoken to Mrs. Havelston, and that is an appointment to have measurements taken and a dress made."

Caroline's hands stopped the work of unfolding the note. She looked at Kitty with wide eyes. "I do not understand. Mrs. Havelston said she refused to serve me."

"She did," Kitty agreed. "But, you are family, and I could not let you be cut off from one of the best modistes in England." She smiled.

Caroline shook her head in disbelief.

"Allow me to explain." Kitty folded her hands in her lap and drew a breath. "As you know, I have four sisters. As I am sure is true for you and your sister, I and mine have not always gotten along. There has been fighting. Hats and gloves have been taken. Hair has been pulled. Names have been called. There have been times when I have wished to be an only child because being compared to and teased by my sisters has been a torment." She smiled at Caroline. "Even Jane, as sweet as she is, can be sharp and unyielding."

Caroline's eyebrows rose. "Surely not."

"I assure you it is entirely possible." She looked down at her hands for a moment. "But no matter the grief they have caused, I love them, and every time they offend, I forgive them." She looked up. "It is not easy, but it is necessary. Do you understand?"

Caroline said that she did, and Kitty continued her explanation just to make certain the point had not been missed. "That appointment is my forgiveness. It is not easily given, but it is necessarily done."

"Thank you," murmured Caroline.

"There is one more thing I should like to give you, but for an entirely different reason." Kitty took out a small notebook and a pencil. "As your friends have guessed, I have sold some of my designs to Mrs. Havelston. Those are reserved for Lady Matlock. However, I would like to design a gown for you."

Caroline shook her head and blinked her eyes rapidly to rid them of the tears that threatened. "I do not deserve it," she whispered.

"No, you do not," agreed Kitty. "But I wish to give it you if you will answer a few questions and then listen to an explanation." Kitty opened the notebook. "Oh, and you must not divulge my name as the designer. Do we have an agreement?"

Caroline nodded.

"Very well. I have noticed that you wear dresses at soirees that have small sleeves and a very straight line. Is this the style of gown you would prefer I create?"

"I feel that they make me look taller."

Kitty nodded and wrote that down. "Do you prefer flounces or lace?"

"Lace."

"Light and flowing or more substantial fabrics."

"Light and flowing. It feels nice to have it swishing so easily while dancing."

Kitty smiled. "I agree. It is much more pleasant. Now, colour, what colour do you prefer?"

"Oh, my friends have told me that I look divine in soft orange. They say it highlights the bits of ginger in my hair."

Kitty tilted her head and bit the top of her pencil. Orange was not a dreadful colour on Miss Bingley. However, it was not the best choice. Did she dare to say so? Yes, today, she must dare to do what she believed was right. "I do not agree. The colours are too similar. They blend. I would think that a blue or green would be more flattering. Either of those colours would show the fairness of your complexion and hair to its best advantage."

"You must be mistaken," Miss Bingley said with a smug look. "Miss Ivison assures me that orange is my best colour, and since both she and I have been in society more than you, Miss Bennet, I think we know more of what is accepted than you do."

Kitty lowered her pencil and leaned forward. One did not have to have travelled in any sort of society whatsoever to know which colour flattered which complexion best, and in this, she would not allow herself to be made to feel inferior, especially since what she knew to be true was something which could help the lady in front of her.

"Miss Bingley, I apologize if you find what I am about to say is offensive, but I think it needs to be said. Miss Ivison is wrong, and I would venture to guess she is purposefully that way."

Miss Bingley gasped. "That cannot be true. Miss Ivison is my friend and would not treat me so shabbily as you suggest."

"How does Miss Ivison treat people who have connections to trade?" Kitty leaned back and folded her arms, watching Miss Bingley shift uneasily in her chair. "I believe I know." Kitty touched her forehead and, again, she let Miss Bingley fidget for a moment before continuing. "You have connections to trade, rather direct ones. Why do you suppose she does not shun you?"

"Because I am an educated and refined lady, not some backwater nobody."

Kitty shook her head as a touch of sorrow pricked her heart about the truth of Miss Bingley's reality. "While your education may give you the refinement necessary to traverse the society in which Miss Ivison circulates, that is not what makes her overcome her distaste for all things related to trade. You have both money and a wealthy brother, who until recently was a single man in possession of a fortune. Though he has married, they have not left you because that would lessen their chances of having some important connections, I would imagine."

Miss Bingley's brows knit together, and she shook her head. "No, they are not like that."

"Then, why did they tell you to wear clothes that would not highlight your beauty? I may not have spent time in town, Miss Bingley, but I assure you that there are petty women in the country. One of them is my sister Lydia. She will tell me a dress looks beautiful on me when I know full well it does not. She does it so that the gentlemen will pay her more attention than me." She laughed bitterly. "And you know, I followed her around and listened to her recommendations even though I knew better." She leaned forward once again. "And do you know why?"

Kitty waited, but Miss Bingley stubbornly refused to answer, so Kitty sighed and continued. "Because I wanted what she had. I wanted to have gentlemen flock to me, and while I followed her directives, I was allowed to stand at her side and comfort those she cast off." Kitty shrugged. "Pathetic, is it not? To follow another just to gain a place in society?"

She picked up her pencil once again. "I will not recommend any fabric that will not look lovely on you because you deserve to find your own place in society. It was Mary who told me to be myself if I wished to capture the colonel's heart, and she was right. You will find that Jane, Mary, and Elizabeth put on no airs when capturing their gentlemen, either."

Miss Bingley's eyes narrowed, and she huffed lightly. "Indeed?"

"Most certainly." Kitty closed her eyes and rubbed her head. Why was sitting and talking such a painful task?

"My place in society has already been chosen." Miss Bingley's voice was as pleasant as Lydia's would be when she wished everyone to think whatever she had to say was pleasing instead of disappointing. "I am to wed Mr. Blackmoore. He will have a baronetcy, you know. One day, I shall be Lady Blackmoore."

Kitty continued to rub her temples but opened her eyes. "He also has a mistress, who will spend all your money and leave the estate in ruin."

Miss Bingley gasped.

"Forgive me, but I think you should know. He has taken up with an actress. He needs a proper wife to secure his inheritance." She shrugged. "Mary told me. Lord Rycroft and Mr. Blackmoore are good friends. You should also know that this actress apparently has an appetite for gaming and a pronounced ability to lose. Hence, my concern for your financial future."

Miss Bingley shoved the paper she still held back at Kitty. "First, you tell me my clothes are not right for my colouring, then you insult my friends, and now, you would speak ill of the man I am to marry. I do not need your appointment. I am certain Lady Blackmoore has connections I can use should I wish to switch modistes."

Kitty tucked her hands under her legs. "I will not take it back. You will go to that appointment. I will design you a dress. And if you should wish it, I will do my best to help you get rid of that actress. No lady, no matter the sins they have committed — and you have committed several — deserves such treatment."

Miss Bingley shrugged. "It is the way of society."

"Not all society." Kitty gave an exasperated sigh. Speaking to Miss Bingley was nearly more taxing than talking to Lydia, and since she knew that speaking to Lydia did little good, she rose. "I fear I have overstayed my time."

She held the back of the chair to steady herself just a bit as the room was once again beginning to spin as it had at Matlock House. "My design will be at Mrs. Havelston's by the day on that card. You have only to ask for it. Good day, Miss Bingley." And with a curtsey, Kitty left Miss Bingley standing there still holding the slip of paper.

Chapter 21

KITTY STOOD FOR A moment outside the door to the room she had just been in. Her head hurt, and so did her heart. Every part of her wanted to dissolve into tears out of utter frustration. But she would not.

"I do not know why I tried to be civil. No, not civil, beyond civil — nice, friendly, generous, forgiving even." Kitty grumbled to Henriella as she walked the length of the hall towards the front door of the Hursts' townhouse.

"Miss Bennet," a surprised Mr. Hurst said as he entered his home. "What brings you calling?"

"A fool's mission, apparently." Kitty covered her mouth with her hand. "Forgive me, I spoke without thought."

What she had said was true, but it was not something that needed to be said. She blamed the spinning of her head for her lack of restraint in allowing her disappointment with both Miss Bingley and herself to be put into words. This was why one should not attempt to do business when one was not feeling well. She should have stayed in bed instead of venturing out. However, the things that needed to be done had been rather urgent. Time, she had thought, was of the essence, and therefore, lying abed had not truly been an option.

Mr. Hurst chuckled. "There is nothing to forgive, Miss Bennet. Caroline is rarely sensible, so you must have been here to call on her."

"I was." Kitty swayed just a bit, and Henriella grabbed her elbow. She would not have fallen over – or at least, she did not think she would have – but the assistance was not unwelcome.

"Perhaps you should sit down and rest for a while until you are feeling more steady," Mr. Hurst said. "You will not have to see Caroline. We will make sure it is a nice quiet room. We can even draw the curtains if you would like the room dark. You really should not be out when you are not well."

Kitty held up her hand to silence his litany of recommendations. "I assure you that I will be well just as soon as I return to my aunt's home and have a rest. Truly, as soon as I am in the carriage and able to close my eyes, the world will stop spinning."

"Are you certain?" He did not look convinced, but truly, she could rest in the carriage as easily, if not more so, than she could in one of the rooms here.

"I will be well. Henriella will see to it that I am." It was far better to feel ill in the comfort of familiar surroundings than to be encouraged to be well in strange rooms, even if the person whose rooms one was in was known to a lady. Kitty rubbed her head. Even her own thoughts were presently causing her pain and making her feel somewhat nauseous.

Mr. Hurst gave her one more questioning look and then extended his arm. "In that case, will you, at least, allow me to help you to your carriage and see you safely seated? It really would do my mind a great service and put it somewhat at ease on your behalf."

She could allow him that act of service, especially if it put his mind at ease, so she placed her hand lightly on the sleeve of his impeccably styled jacket and allowed him to guide her out the door, down the steps, and into her uncle's carriage. She did not know him well, but he seemed rather kind for being married to Miss Bingley's sister. She would wonder if it was just Miss Bingley who was unkind, but she knew Mrs. Hurst's tongue was also sharp. Therefore, she almost felt as if she should feel sorry for Mr. Hurst. A kind person would have a dreadfully difficult time living happily with an unkind person, would they not? Maybe that was why Mr. Hurst seemed to often distance himself from his wife and sister-in-law.

All these thoughts tumbled around each other in a clumsy array as Kitty made her way to her seat in the carriage.

"Miss Bennet," Mr. Hurst said as she settled onto the bench. "Why did you call on my sister?"

That was an excellent question, and one that she was feeling quite keenly. Kitty shrugged. It had seemed like such a good idea when she had come up with it, and if she were to think on it more, she would likely discover that, regardless of the outcome, it had been the right thing to do. She was certain Mary would say so.

"I wished to forgive her for all she has done to me and my sisters," Kitty answered, "and I wanted her to have a tangible representation of that forgiveness." She sighed and, beyond logical reason, hoped that Miss Bingley would still accept the dress.

"You did? May I inquire as to what the gift you offered was?"

"I arranged an appointment with the modiste whose shop she was at when the incident," she touched her forehead, "occurred. I have also promised her a dress of my own design, which is something that no one else is to have, save for Lady Matlock."

"And she refused?" Mr. Hurst could not contain his surprise. "She deserves no such treatment I assure you." His tone was censorious. "You are far too generous."

Kitty did not feel like she deserved such praise. "She did not refuse until I overstepped my bounds. I was perhaps a bit too open with her regarding what I know about Mr. Blackmoore and my opinion of her friends."

"Ah." The word was drawn out as if everything was now perfectly clear to Mr. Hurst. "That does sound like Caroline," he said with a nod. "She does value her connections quite highly – too highly in this case. I am sorry for the injury she has caused you and for her apparent ingratitude for your forgiveness. I trust you will be well soon."

"Thank you, Mr. Hurst."

He paused in closing the door. "You will be well?"

"Henriella will see to it that I am, will you not?"

"Of course, miss."

Mr. Hurst drew a noticeable breath and then, with a nod, closed the door and tapped on the side of the vehicle.

Kitty waved to him through the window as the carriage lurched forward. He stood there, watching, until she could not seem him any longer. She had never thought that someone who dressed so fashionably and carried himself with an air of not wishing to be anywhere he was, could be anxious and attentive. Silently, as she rested her head against the back of the carriage, she wondered if it was that attentiveness or just his fortune and fashion sense that had drawn Mrs. Hurst to him.

She closed her eyes. She had done what she had determined she would do upon waking this morning. Unfortunately, not all her plans had ended successfully. At least, the meeting with Lord Matlock had gone better than the one with Miss Bingley.

She popped her head up as something Lord Matlock had said came to mind. "Henriella, do you suppose Thomas would buy a paper for me?" She searched inside her reticule for the amount she would need for the purchase.

Henriella knocked on the roof of the carriage, and soon, they had stopped, and the door opened. "A paper for Miss Bennet," she instructed as she handed the coins Kitty had found to Thomas.

Thomas stared at the money. "But there is not a paper to be purchased here, and it is rather late to be procuring one."

"There must be one boy or another who is desperate to sell what remains of his copies," Henriella returned. "Climb back up on the box and keep a close eye, so that we can stop and purchase the first one you see." Though she was giving commands, there was a pleasantness to her tone, for she was never truly harsh with her brother.

"As you wish," Thomas said. "Miss Bennet, I am sure it will not be too long until I find a paper for you. Or I should say, I hope it is not."

"Thank you, Thomas. All I ask is that you do your best, for I wish to know why Lord Matlock asked if I had read the paper. I really must start reading it in the mornings. If I had, this gash might not be on my head and the world would stand still instead of wobbling about like the colourful jelly at the end of a fine meal."

"I will do my best, miss."

Thomas closed the door, and they continued on their way for some distance before stopping once again.

"Did you find a paper?" Kitty asked when the door opened. "That was very fast – Oh!" she said when she realized that the person at the door was not her uncle's footman but Richard. "I had need of a paper," she explained. "Your father seemed to think it is important that I read it."

"Pardon me, Colonel. I would like to stretch my legs," Henriella said as she moved to exit the carriage. "I will take Thomas with me, miss," she added as Richard helped her from the carriage.

"You might want to look in that direction," Richard said as he pointed to his left.

Once Henriella had scurried off with a call to Thomas to attend her, Richard climbed into the vehicle, took a seat across from Kitty, and closed the door. Then, with a tap on the roof, the carriage began moving.

"Wait! What about Henriella?" Kitty looked out the window in desperation.

"Darcy will see that she and Thomas are returned to the Gardiners'." He moved across to sit next to her.

"Mr. Darcy?" Kitty glanced out the window. "I do not see him."

"I pointed your maid in the direction of his carriage. She will be fine."

"Are you certain? She has taken such good care of me that I would hate for her to be left behind."

"Shhh, my love." He took her hand. "Your maid will be well. I would like to hear about your day. I know that you have been to see my father, and I assume that you are in Mayfair to see Mr. Hurst?"

She shook her head slightly and grimaced. "I came to see Miss Bingley." She closed her eyes and found herself gathered to him with her head pressed against his shoulder.

"I would dearly like to know why, but I do not wish to tax you further. You must be exhausted."

"I am, but if you allow me to rest my head here and speak with my eyes closed, I shall attempt an explanation." And she did. She told him everything from the visit to Mrs. Havelston to the conference with his father and finally, to her call on Miss Bingley.

He stroked her hair as she spoke. The soothing action caused her words to begin to slur as she ended her tale.

"But I do not know why your father wished for me to read the paper or why he insisted that you are to marry me and not Miss de Bourgh."

"Shh," he said as he continued to run his hand along her hair. "There is an explanation, but it would be best if you were rested before I give it. I promise you will know everything as soon as you are rested."

She opened her eyes halfway and smiled at him. She was very fortunate to be loved by such a compassionate man.

He kissed the top of her head. "Just know for now that I will indeed be marrying you and not my cousin Anne."

"You will?" It was not as if she expected him to lie to her, but it was so wonderful a thing that she needed to hear again that it was true.

"I will."

The news made her heart and her lips sigh with delight. He was hers, and she was his.

He kissed her head again. "Rest, my love. All is well," he whispered. "All is well."

Chapter 22

JANUARY 21, 1812

THE SUN PUSHED ITS way over the horizon, etching fingers of colour across the frosted glass of the window and, at long last, giving Kitty permission to rise and stretch. She had lain, snuggled under the warmth of her blankets, for an hour, just waiting for this moment. She knew that now, though her room was chilly, there would be a fire burning in the dining room and her uncle would be there, reading his paper, sipping his tea, and finishing his toast before he left for his warehouse. Now was the perfect time to venture forth from her room. Earlier would not have been.

The anxious fluttering in her stomach, which had greeted her before the sun had, increased as she sat on the side of her bed and looked at the ball gown that hung on her wardrobe door. Tonight, she would be presented to London society as the future Mrs. Richard Fitzwilliam.

She giggled as she rubbed her arms to warm them. It still sounded strange to her to call him Mr. Fitzwilliam instead of Colonel, but at Admiral Fitzwilliam's insistence, a substitute had quickly been found to complete Richard's term in the militia, a situation that pleased Richard but left his father less than happy. Seeing that Lord Matlock was often disgruntled seemed to be the new purpose of Admiral Fitzwilliam's life. As far as Kitty was concerned, her future father-in-law deserved the discomfort. He was, as Mary liked to say, only reaping what he had sown. Truly, Kitty was just glad that her colonel would be able to chart his own future and that she would be able to be at his side whether Lord Matlock found that to his liking or not.

Having done the few things necessary to make herself comfortable and presentable – the rest could be done once the room was warmed and water was not so frigid, Kitty stuffed her feet into her slippers and tied her robe tightly around herself before scooting out the door and down the stairs.

"Your paper." Uncle Gardiner handed her the paper as she entered the room. He had already opened it and folded it to the page that showed the important society happenings, such as engagements. "I see no notice declaring you have broken your agreement with Fitzwilliam. I believe you may rest easy."

She smiled at his tease. But it had been those announcements – the ones about which she did not know until they were sprung upon her – which had started her reading the paper first thing in the morning. Now, however, she did it to be well-versed in all the happenings of town. She was determined that in that area, at least, Miss Bingley and her friends would never again find her wanting.

She scanned the announcements and stopped to read a few of the *on dits* so that she was aware of what was what and who was tied to whom in society. This was important information for venturing forth and not looking like a simpleton from the country. It would also help her know about what Lady Matlock was talking, for Richard's mother did enjoy a tantalizing story.

Then, she flipped the paper around to read the news. This part she read to be well-versed on topics of conversation she might hear between the men of her new family.

"Ladies do not read the news," her uncle said with a chuckle.

"Ladies do read the news," she retorted. She knew Lady Sophia did. "They just refuse to speak about it when gentlemen are around for fear the gentlemen might feel threatened."

Her uncle laughed aloud at that and said, "Well, now, I dare say most of us would not be threatened by an intelligent woman."

"That is not what Mama says," Kitty replied with a smile.

"Ah, it is good to hear arguing and merriment in the room," her aunt said as she entered. "You were so sullen and quiet when you came home with us from Longbourn after Jane's and Mary's weddings. You were certainly not the Kitty I knew." As she took her seat, she held up a hand to stop the protest that Kitty was prepared to make.

"I know, you feel as though you have never really been yourself, and that you were rather an actress trying to find her role; however, you know I disagree."

And strongly! Aunt Gardiner had been very vocal about her opinion on that matter.

"You may have been led to do things or behave certain ways by your sister," her aunt continued, "but I remember you as a young child, and sullen is not a word I would ever use to describe the child you were. You were happy, stubborn, and sweet."

She poured a cup of tea and chuckled as she reached for a roll and added, "There is not a one of you girls who is not stubborn to some degree, but then, most of the women in this family have an obstinate bent, whether they are related through blood or just marriage." She winked at her husband, who grinned.

"I will not argue against that, but I will add that they all have their own wonderful sweetness."

"Well said, my dear," Aunt Gardiner said with a laugh before turning back to Kitty.

"You know," she began as she broke the roll apart and prepared to eat it, "I remember on one of my visits to Longbourn, when you were no more than five, you had found a bird hopping around the yard and were determined to catch it. You giggled and giggled and giggled as you chased it until the whole of the garden was filled with your mirth. But then, you caught it."

She shook her head. "And discovered that the poor creature was hopping because it could not fly. Of course, because you could not bear to see another in pain, even if it was a bird, you insisted that it be cared for. Your father was not so certain that it was necessary to tend to an injured bird." Aunt Gardiner tsked. "Oh my, the tears that fell until your father relented!"

She chuckled softly as she lifted her roll, but before she took a bite, she added, "That is who you are – Katherine Bennet, a pleasant young woman who has great determination and a heart that is as soft and sweet as the fresh cream on this bun."

Mr. Gardiner rose and took the paper back from Kitty. "And I have found it wisest to always agree with everything your aunt says." He winked at her and then kissed his wife's cheek before heading to his warehouse.

It was lovely to hear herself spoken of in such a way. She hoped that she could always be the person her aunt described.

Mrs. Gardiner moved from roll to teacup. "How is your head this morning?"

"I have not had a dizzy spell since," she bit her lip and contemplated how long it had been, "since the day before yesterday." There had not even been more than a small headache yesterday.

"Good. Be sure that you are not too active today if you wish to survive the evening. In fact, a rest this afternoon before you dress would be beneficial. I am sure Mary would be willing to allow for that." She clucked her tongue. "I am still unwilling to forgive your little adventure around town so shortly after your injury." Her brows rose, and she looked over her cup at her niece. "But I think you have learned from the experience, have you not?"

Kitty smiled sheepishly. She remembered well the scolding she had received, first from her aunt and then, from the surgeon, after she had returned from her visit to Miss Bingley's house. "I have been good for more than two weeks, Aunt."

And it was true. She had kept mostly to the house. She had only left the house on short excursions with her aunt to a shop or with Richard for a walk. Even at home her activities had been few. Stitching and drawing had proven to be ones that would make her head throb more quickly than simply sitting and listening, sometimes with eyes closed, to the conversation in the room or to a passage being read.

Thankfully, Richard had been obliging and had called often to keep her company. He was a wonderful conversationalist, and Kitty was never so content as she was when he sat beside her reading to her and holding her hand.

Her aunt's teacup clattered just a bit as it was returned to its saucer, interrupting Kitty's reverie. "Well, see that you continue to be so." It might have been a harsh comment had it not been accompanied by a pat of the hand and a smile.

Kitty and her aunt lapsed into a comfortable silence that was broken only by the occasional comment from her aunt regarding some item that needed attention. There were menus to finalize, an order for the larder that needed review before it was sent, and one of Uncle's shirts that needed a quick mend, amongst other tasks.

When her tea was finished, Kitty rose to go back to her room.

"Will you be ready to go in an hour?" her aunt asked.

They were to spend the day with Mary and her sisters at Rycroft Place before the ball that was planned for that evening.

"I can be," Kitty answered, but then, remembering the comments her aunt had made as they ate, added, "But will that give you time to do what is needed? We can leave later if necessary."

"Oh, my dear, yes. I will have plenty of time, and I have no desire to postpone one bit of this day. I think I am more excited about this ball than you." A smile of pure delight lit her aunt's face. "It is not every tradesman's wife who is invited to Rycroft Place to attend a soiree with people the likes of Lord and Lady Matlock."

Kitty's shoulders drooped just a bit. Lord Matlock was still just as arrogant and rude as she had ever known him to be. The admiral or a mention of the admiral kept him from truly puffing himself up, but he was still excessively pompous. There was little hope that he would not say something about her aunt and uncle's social standing tonight. The thought hurt her heart.

As if reading her mind, Aunt Gardiner waved Kitty away. "I know what people of their station think of me, my dear. It will come as no shock if I am shunned. But to see the splendor of it all..." she sighed. "It will be quite the treat."

She rose and wiped her hands on her apron. "Now, for my first task – to see to the children before I leave them with their nurse for the day." She hurried out of the room. "And then, I shall see to the needs in the kitchen before mending that shirt." This was all tossed over her shoulder as she climbed the stairs.

Kitty laughed at her aunt's exuberance as she followed behind her at a more sedate pace. Although Kitty wished to rush up the stairs to prepare for the day, just as her aunt was doing, there was the hint of a small pain above her eye that lingered and made her refrain. She had no time to nurse her head today because she had been foolish.

Tonight, she would be expected to smile, converse, and dance, at least once, which were all things she could do more easily if her head did not hurt, and she did not want to miss out on any of them. However, more than the pain and fatigue that she knew would accompany any overexertion which would make being charming an excruciating challenge, the thought of missing her chance to dance with Richard made her willing to move slowly and to rest when she would rather not, for the dearness of the reward was well-worth the price.

Chapter 23

"Miss Bennet."

Kitty turned toward the sound of the voice but saw no one. The dancing had begun, and having had her first dance with her betrothed, she was now sitting in a quiet corner, waiting for a cup of lemonade to be brought to her.

"Miss Bennet."

Again, Kitty turned toward the voice. "Miss de Bourgh, I can hear you, but I am afraid I cannot see you."

"Behind the plant."

"Oh." Kitty turned, and there, behind a couple of tall potted plants, was Anne.

"Please, do not look at me."

Kitty turned back around. "Very well, but I shall look foolish speaking to myself, and someone might come to investigate." Anne reminded Kitty a bit of Lydia – she was stubborn as a grumpy old donkey, and rather nonsensical at times – such as now.

"I only wish to know if a certain gentleman is occupied." There was a bit of a rustling from behind Kitty. "You would not believe the number of gentlemen who have come to call, and I have had at least ten requests for a dance this evening."

"That is to be expected when one places an advertisement for a husband and declares herself an heiress." Richard took the seat next to Kitty while looking toward his cousin, who was now only partially concealed by the plants. "You look lovely this evening, Anne. No need to hide."

Kitty laughed at the small growling sound that came from behind her.

"Mr. Blackmoore. Is he occupied?"

"Yes, he has engaged Miss Bingley for a dance."

Anne slipped out from behind the plant. "He has called four times this week, wishing to meet with me. I saw him once and told him he had no hope of gaining my approval."

She flipped open her fan and whispered behind it. "He has taken up with an actress, I hear." She tsked. "And I told him, he would not succeed because of it; however, he seems most determined tonight to lead me off into a dark corner."

She scanned the room. "He would be better off with that Bingley woman. Horrible thing she is. Such a ghastly colour she wears, and her airs... as if she were of a standing to be making any."

"I did not know you knew Miss Bingley," Kitty said in surprise.

Anne shrugged. "I do not know her beyond what I have seen this evening and what my uncle has shared of her family, but that is enough." She turned toward Kitty. "Now, if she were a gentleman's daughter as you are, even if she, like you, were of little standing, her airs could be borne. But as it is…" She shook her head. "She makes a fool of herself."

Richard cleared his throat and gave his cousin a pointed glare.

Anne looked at him in confusion. "Have I said something amiss again?"

He nodded, and Anne sighed loudly.

"My mother really did do me a disservice by not allowing me to venture into society beyond what can be found in Kent. Do tell me what I have said."

Kitty placed a hand on Anne's arm. "A lady, unless she is Miss Bingley or one of her friends, does not point out another lady's lower circumstances. However, I know you were not doing so to be injurious to me, but rather simply stating facts. The same will not be true when speaking to other ladies."

Anne closed her fan and took Kitty's hand. "Oh! I am so very sorry, my dear. I like you, you know. Very much." She giggled. "And not just because doing so holds the potential to irk my mother and uncle, but because I like you."

She scanned the room once more. "My mother appears to be engaged. I think I shall find Lord Rycroft and seek an introduction to the gentleman to whom he is speaking."

"Lord Brownlow is a fine choice," Kitty said with a smile as she saw Anne making her way toward the gentleman.

"Much better than Blackmoore," muttered Richard. "I do hope she stays out of dark corners. I would not think Blackmoore above causing a compromise to attain her money and connections." He chuckled. "It would be entertaining, however, to see him matching wills with my cousin."

Kitty gave his arm a light swat and shook her head in amusement.

"Come." Richard captured the hand that hit him and drew her to her feet. "Let's take a turn of the room." He tucked her hand in the crook of his arm but then, paused to give her a searching look.

"I am well," she assured him. "And I have promised my sisters and aunt, as well as Lord Rycroft and Mr. Darcy, that I will steal away for a rest if I should need it."

Noting how his attention seemed to be captured by her wound, she rubbed his arm under her hand reassuringly. "It hurts a little, but as long as I am not turning circles in a dance, the room stands still." She squeezed one eye closed as it seemed to help lessen the small stabbing pains that affected her less frequently than they had at first. "Perhaps we should just walk the edges of the room that are furthest from the musicians?"

He covered her hand with his. "We could steal away together. Rycroft would not mind lending us the use of his study."

She smiled up at him. "As lovely as that sounds, we cannot. I will not have your father thinking of me as a hoyden. It is enough that my uncle is in trade. I do not wish to give him any more reasons to dislike me."

Richard chuckled. "I think, my dear, that he was quite impressed by your visit. He may even like you already."

Kitty shook her head. "That is doubtful. I attempted to blackmail him into giving you your freedom."

"That would be one way to impress a man like my father. He is not above coercion to attain what he desires." He led her down the edge of the ballroom. "He has mentioned you several times since your visit, and always with a *surprising woman* somewhere in the conversation."

"I do not know if that pleases me or not."

They had reached the end of the room and stood next to the very person about whom they had been speaking.

"Ah, Miss Bennet." Lord Matlock gave her a small bow and what she assumed was a pleased smile, although it was hard to say for sure as it was such a fleeting expression. "I trust you are well this evening."

"I am, thank you, my lord." She curtsied. "You appear to also be well."

He preened just a bit at her comment and smoothed the front of his waistcoat before tugging at it to make the buttons form a straight line. "My wife has insisted that some part of my attire match her dress. It is silly, but I did not wish to displease her." He nodded toward where his wife was talking to a group of ladies that included Lady Catherine. "Is that one of the sketches you showed me?"

Kitty nodded. "It is, my lord. It looks quite lovely on Lady Matlock, and that colour is rather heavenly, do you not think?"

"Oh, indeed. My lady does have an eye for colour. Always has." He looked around the room as if searching for someone. "Your aunt is here?"

Kitty did not miss the slight twitch of his lips as if he had not wished to speak of the subject.

"She is, but you do not have to meet her. She is aware of her low standing and will not be offended." She gave the arm that had tightened under her hand a calming squeeze. "It is enough for her to just be here and to take in the spectacle. In fact, meeting someone of such an elevated position as yourself may prove to be too much for her. I would fear she would never recover from such an honour."

Lord Matlock puffed out his chest just a bit more and smoothed his waistcoat once again, and Richard coughed, likely to cover a laugh from the amusement in his eyes.

"Your uncle is in which livery?"

"He is a Mercer, my lord."

"Ah, a high precedence." Lord Matlock's brows rose, and his lower lip stuck out just a bit as he bobbed his head as if this information pleased him. "If it would not tax your aunt too greatly, I would not be opposed to an introduction."

"You do my family a great honour, my lord." She gave a small curtsey. "However, I must first speak with my sister, Mrs. Darcy." Who was approaching them.

Lord Matlock nodded. "Perhaps after supper?"

"If you wish, my lord." She gave one more small curtsey, which caused him to fleetingly smile that smile of approval, and breathed a sigh of relief as they moved away.

"How do you know how to speak to him in such a fashion?" Richard asked softly when they were well away from his father.

Kitty shrugged. "It is no different than speaking to Aunt Philips and Mrs. Long. They like to feel their importance whether it is real or imagined."

"Why are you speaking about our aunt?" Elizabeth queried as she slid her arm through Kitty's free one.

"Katherine seems to be an expert at dealing with my father," Richard explained, "and I wished to know how she learned such a skill. She said she acquired it from dealing with your aunt." He looked over his shoulder toward where Lord Matlock stood. "My father is still looking well-satisfied with himself."

"So, he is," Elizabeth said with a laugh. "You will have to tell me how you do it. I am certain he will never look so pleased after speaking to me."

"It is not so very hard," Kitty said, "but I will show you if you wish." It was pleasant to think that she had something she could teach Elizabeth. "Do you think it would be possible for us to find a place to rest?" Kitty asked her sister.

"Are you unwell?" Concern etched Richard's face.

"I am a bit tired is all."

"Good," said Elizabeth. "Oh, not that you are tired, but that you wish to rest, for I also would like to find some solitude. However, if I sneak off to the library with my husband alone, tongues will wag more than they already do."

Kitty removed her arm from Richard's and moved toward the library with her sister.

"You gentlemen may join us, of course," Elizabeth said to Darcy with a nod toward Richard. Then she leaned toward her sister and whispered. "I am not well, but no one must know, at least not yet."

"What do you mean?"

"I may be with child."

Kitty's eyes grew large. "Are you certain?"

Elizabeth shook her head. "Not completely, but it appears to be true. You mustn't tell anyone, but I could not keep it to myself any longer, and with your injury requiring that you rest, I had hoped you might aid me by providing me with a reason to rest more frequently."

"Of course, I would be happy to oblige if that is what you wish."

"Are you surprised by my request?"

"Not the request, but by the fact that you told me. You never tell me secrets."

Elizabeth pulled Kitty closer. "I am sorry. I plan to change that."

"You need not apologize. Being surprised does not mean I am not pleased. I am. Very, very pleased." She glanced over her shoulder to make certain the gentlemen were not too close to hear. "When will you tell Mr. Darcy?"

"I have not decided. I would like to share it with him, but if I am wrong..." She bit her lip and did not continue. "I would rather be certain."

Kitty squeezed her arm. "I will not say a word, and I will offer chances to rest whenever you may need them."

"Thank you," Elizabeth said as a footman opened the library door for them. "Now, I do not wish to desert you, but Darcy has insisted that we find a place to read." Her eyebrows waggled just a bit and her cheeks coloured.

Kitty smiled. "I hear poetry is the food of a fine, stout love."

Elizabeth laughed. "I have heard that as well," she said as the two sisters parted.

Kitty took a slow turn around the room admiring the tables and chairs and stopping to feel the fabric of the drapery. "It is all so lovely," she muttered. "The colours and the design complement each other perfectly."

"Lady Sophia has an excellent eye. This was her doing." Richard took her by the arm and led her to an alcove with a comfortable seat. "You said you were in need of a rest, and this looks like just the spot for it," he explained, taking a seat next to her. "We will not have anything this fine. BayLeafe is only a small estate."

"I am quite happy with a modest estate, my love. It is what I have always known." She peeked up at him. "Will you be happy? You could have married for convenience and had something far grander."

He pulled her close. "I am quite happy with my inconvenient choice," he teased as he ran a finger across the scar on her forehead and then cupped her cheek in his hand. "I am not romantic, so I fear my terms of endearment might not always be what one might expect."

She smiled up at him. Although he kept saying that he was not romantic, she knew differently. He may not be given to romantic, flowery, loving words, but when he pulled her slightly closer as they walked the streets of London, when he brought her a box engraved with forget-me-knots for her pencils, and when he rubbed her cheek with his thumb as he did now, his actions spoke in thunderous tones of his love.

"I do not require a romantic," she said, pressing her cheek more firmly into his hand. "I require only you."

"And I, you." He kissed the scar on her forehead. "I love you, Katherine Bennet." He kissed the scar once again. "Two days," he whispered. "Two days and you shall be mine."

"I already am," she replied.

"From the moment we met," he agreed.

His thumb continued to caress her cheek as he tilted his head to study her face. She kissed his thumb as it brushed over her lips, causing him to inhale sharply. Sliding his hand around to the back of her head, he drew her to him for a kiss that was, at first, soft and sweet, speaking of the treasure she was to him. But then, as he drew her even closer, the kiss deepened, showing her his need to have her by his side.

When finally, he broke the kiss and leaned his forehead against hers, he whispered, "You will always be my choice. Before money, before connections, before anyone or anything, it will be you. I will always choose you."

"And I, you," she said as she rested her head on his shoulder and her hand on his heart, a heart that would always be hers. Through happy times and times of sorrow, from meager beginnings to days of plenty, it would beat for her just as hers beat for him.

Theirs was a love that would be spoken of in corners of drawing rooms and behind fans at balls, not for its passion, though there was plenty, nor for its demonstrative nature, though their hands were often joined in public, but for its quiet assurance and its unbreakable bonds. It was a love that would eventually win over even their harshest critic, making Lord Matlock into a doting grandfather.

And Richard, when asked to tell of his good fortune — for he would become as sought after for his wooden creations as his wife would be for her designs — would smile, lift Kitty's hand to his lips, and begin each reply with an "Ah, yes, my inconvenient choice."

If you enjoyed this book, be sure to let others know by leaving a review.

~*~*~

Want to know when other Leenie books will be available?
You can always know what's new with my books by subscribing to my mailing list.

leeniebrown.com/subscribe

~*~*~

Turn the page to read an excerpt of another one of Leenie's books.

Her Heart's Choice

Excerpt

PROLOGUE

JANUARY 9, 1812

Alexander Madoch tossed the newspaper on the table and tapped the section he wished his friend Jonathan Lester to read before picking up a hunk of cheese and popping it into his mouth. He rose from his chair and walked to the window that overlooked the street. Two horses, wearing the colours of his uncle's stable, carried a pair of finely dressed women toward the beach. The ladies were not alone, however, as a group of young men followed close behind. He smiled as he watched the positioning of the gentlemen shift, one nudging the other out of the way to get closer to one or the other of the ladies.

"So the little termagant has decided to marry," said Jonathan, drawing Alex's attention back to the room. "I feel sorry for the chap that has to put up with her."

Alex turned from the window. "That chap shall be me. It seems we must make a trip to London."

"You? After the way she turned you out?" Jonathan shook his head and scowled. "I'd not be chasing after the likes of her again. Be gone and good riddance, I would say."

Alex turned back to the window. A young man was finally riding next to one of the young ladies. They were a good distance off, but still Alex could see how the young woman turned to the gentleman and slowed to allow him to ride more fully at her side. Alex bit his lip and tilted his head as he watched the pair ride away. That was what he had wanted those many years ago. A lady, a particular lady, to ride away with him. "She was not wrong in her refusal," he said without turning toward his friend.

Jonathan huffed his disagreement.

"The risk truly was too great. I had no guarantee of success."

"You also had no guarantee of failure." Jonathan pushed the paper away from where it lay in front of him. "As I see it, you had only to increase in your standing. Anyone admitted to your confidence knows how hard you work and how you do not venture unless there is a very promising chance of success."

Alex remained looking out the window. It would do no good to argue the point with his friend, for he had wholeheartedly agreed with such a sentiment at first. In fact, if he allowed himself to consider it, he still felt somewhat bitter over the fact that she had not believed enough in his success to accept him. "I did fall into some wonderful chances that I did not expect." He chuckled slightly as he turned toward his friend. "Wouldn't she be surprised to learn of my connection to Prinny?" He had not expected his uncle to have been the one to help Prince George find his Brighton retreat, nor had he expected his uncle to recommend him as manager of the Prince Regent's riding school and stables. His friend had also benefitted as Alex has engaged him as a man of business and assistant in his duties to the prince.

"That would put an end to her argument of your lack of connections," Jonathan agreed.

Alex began to nod his agreement but then shifted it to a shake of his head. "No." His head shook from side to side with more determination. "She is not to know of my connections. Not a one of them beyond those I have through my uncle."

Jonathan's countenance told of his lack of understanding.

"I need her to accept me. Not my money and not my connections. I will have her as a wife, but only if she accepts me without all of those accoutrements." His right hand circled in the air as if fluffing something.

Jonathan pulled the paper back to him. "Did you read this? She has required that all potential suitors have, and I quote 'in their possession a title as well as solvent and accurate financial reports' and..." He held up a finger to emphasise his point. "'Please be advised that references and documentation showing adherence to the above criteria will be required.' Exactly how to you propose to gain an audience with her majesty when you do not have a title and are unwilling to mention your connections."

Alex crossed the room and opened the door to call to the butler, giving him instructions to see that all was made ready for his trip. Then, with a smile, he turned to his friend. "How have I always gained an audience where none was extended?"

Jonathan groaned. "Who am I to write about soirees?"

"Do you still correspond with Brownlow?"

"On occasion, but that is a business matter and this..." he waved at the paper as he rose to follow his friend from the room.

"Is a business matter," said Alex. "Your job is to see that I make all the proper connections, that all the required meetings are arranged so that I might be able to be successful in my ventures, is it not?"

His friend sighed and shook his head. "This is not a business venture, but I shall give you every opportunity I can arrange. However, I am still not in favour of the idea."

Alex clapped his friend on the shoulder. "As far as I am concerned, my friend, this is the most important business venture in which you will ever take part. That is, of course, until you find yourself a woman to pursue in earnest."

Jonathan groaned once again as they left the dining room.

Alex stopped abruptly and turned to face his friend. "We must not fail in this venture." He placed a hand on each of Jonathan's shoulders. "We simply cannot fail."

His friend sighed. "Very well. I can see the importance, and I will do my best to help secure her. Though I question your sanity, I will do it for you."

"Thank you. That is all that I ask." A smile lit his face. "Now, to tell my uncle that I shall be leaving for town in two days." He let out a great breath as if being relieved of some great burden as he exited the house. Indeed, he had not felt such welcome vigour in some time. He had no doubt that the challenge that lay before him would tax him to the end of his patience. She always had. But, he drew a deep, satisfying breath as he walked toward the stables, the prize — ah, the prize for endurance would be satisfying indeed. Finally, his heart would feel whole.

About Leenie

Leenie Brown has always been a girl with an active imagination, which, while growing up, was both an asset, providing many hours of fun as she played out stories, and a liability, when her older sister and aunt would tell her frightening tales. At one time, they had her convinced Dracula lived in the trunk at the end of the bed she slept in when visiting her grandparents!

Although it has been years since she cowered in her bed in her grandparents' basement, she still has an imagination which occasionally runs away with her, and she feeds it now as she did then — by reading!

Her heroes, when growing up, were authors, and the worlds they painted with words were (and still are) her favourite playgrounds! Now, as an adult, she spends much of her time in the Regency world, playing with the characters from her favourite Jane Austen novels and those of her own creation.

When she is not traipsing down a trail in an attempt to keep up with her imagination, Leenie resides in the beautiful province of Nova Scotia with her two sons and her very own Mr. Brown (a wonderful mix of all the best of Darcy, Bingley, and Edmund with a healthy dose of the teasing Mr. Tilney and just a dash of the scolding Mr. Knightley).

More Books by Leenie

You can find all of Leenie's books at this link

bit.ly/LeenieBBooks
where you can explore the collections below
~*~

Dash of Darcy and Companions Collection

Marrying Elizabeth Series

Sweet Possibilities and Sweet Extras

Willow Hall Romances

The Choices Series

Darcy Family Holidays

Darcy and... An Austen-Inspired Collection

Teatime Tales (Sweet Austen-inspired Novelettes)

Other Pens

Touches of Austen

Nature's Fury and Delights (Sweet Regency Novelettes)

Connect with Leenie

Subscribe to Leenie's Mailing List:

leeniebrown.com/subscribe
Website:

leeniebrown.com
Patreon:

patreon.com/LeenieBrown
Facebook:

facebook.com/LeenieBrownAuthor
MeWe:

mewe.com/p/leeniebrown1
Instagram:

@leenie.b (Leenie B Books)
E-mail: LeenieBrownAuthor@gmail.com